W9-DCL-733

Rae snatched her fingers away from the sheet of paper as if it were on fire. But the thoughts kept coming.

YOU NEED TO BE BACK IN THIS HOSPITAL. SAFE IN YOUR OWN LITTLE ROOM. STRAPPED IN YOUR OWN LITTLE BED.

Those thoughts aren't coming from fingerprints, Rae thought. *And they aren't coming from me. They aren't.*

But wasn't that what all lunatics thought? That the voices in their heads were from God or dogs or aliens or something?

Have I been crazy all this time? Am I going to end up in here for the rest of my life? Rae was sure those thoughts were her own. And they froze the blood in her veins.

[redacted]

Don't miss any of the books in this
thrilling new series:

fingerprints

#1: Gifted Touch
#2: Haunted
#3: Trust Me
#4: Secrets
#5: Betrayed
#6: Revelations
#7: Payback

[redacted]

fingerprints™ 7

payback

melinda metz

AVON BOOKS
An Imprint of HarperCollins*Publishers*

Payback

Copyright © 2002 by 17th Street Productions, an Alloy, Inc. company, and Melinda Metz.

All rights reserved. No part of this book may be used or reproduced in any manner whatsoever without written permission except in the case of brief quotations embodied in critical articles or reviews.

Printed in the United States of America.

For information address
HarperCollins Children's Books, a division of
HarperCollins Publishers, 1350 Avenue of the Americas,
New York, NY 10019.

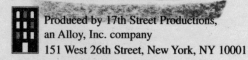

Produced by 17th Street Productions,
an Alloy, Inc. company
151 West 26th Street, New York, NY 10001

Library of Congress Catalog Card Number: 2001118040
ISBN 0-06-000620-X

First Avon edition, 2002

AVON TRADEMARK REG. U.S. PAT. OFF.
AND IN OTHER COUNTRIES,
MARCA REGISTRADA, HECHO EN U.S.A.

Visit us on the World Wide Web!
www.harperteen.com

For my friend Sara Dager

payback

Chapter 1

Rae Voight had an impulse to stop dead in the middle of the hallway, fling her arms out wide, and cry, "Just look, okay? Just take a good long look and stop giving me all those sneaky, out-of-the-corner-of-your-eye glances."

But she didn't. When everyone at school recently found out your mother was a murderer who died in a mental hospital and everyone already knew that you had spent your summer vacation in, yes, a mental hospital, it wasn't that smart to draw *more* attention to yourself.

Except . . . at this point, all of that barely seemed to matter. How bizarre was that? The possibility that even her best friend might find out the truth about Rae's mom used to be Rae's biggest fear. And now everybody knew.

She was sure even the janitor had heard. She was sure the AV guys, who usually didn't talk about anything except how bad they wanted a plasma TV, were gossiping about her. And she cared . . . some. That's it. She wasn't even close to being destroyed the way she'd always thought she would be if anyone found out about her mom.

Maybe it was because she knew her mother hadn't killed anyone. She'd been convinced of that ever since she'd touched a letter with her mother's fingerprints on it and used her psychic ability to pick up the thoughts her mom had been having when she wrote the letter. But now she had proof—Aiden's confession. Aiden had finally admitted to Rae that her mom had been set up to take the blame for her best friend's death. Rae wasn't the daughter of a killer.

And she also wasn't being stalked by her *own* best friend anymore. Yana Savari had turned out to be the one after her all along, but now Aiden had Yana tucked away somewhere where she couldn't hurt Rae.

So her mom was innocent, and Rae was safe. But even with all of that, the other major reason why Rae didn't really care what anyone here in school thought of her was that Anthony Fascinelli had kissed her—kissed her until her lips got all puffy and sore in a good way. Who could care about anything after that? The kiss hadn't even been after a crisis situation, either. He hadn't kissed her because she'd almost died. Or because he almost had. So it totally counted. A little smile broke across Rae's face as she thought about the kiss and all the kisses that had come after that kiss in the past week. The smile earned her a few more what's-your-deal looks. Clearly people thought Rae should never smile again now that the so-called truth about her mom was out. But forget them. She had to smile. Because school was over for the day, and as soon as she found Anthony, they'd be kissing again.

As if her thoughts had conjured him up, Rae felt Anthony's hands slide around her waist. She twisted around to face him, impatient to feel his mouth on hers, to become RaeAnthony instead of Rae and Anthony. They'd kissed hundreds of times in the week since *the* kiss, but Rae still felt starved for the taste of him. When his lips met hers, God, it was like everything she'd ever wanted in her whole life had been dumped in a pile at her feet with a big bow and whipped cream and a cherry on top.

"Car," Anthony said into her mouth, and he started backing her down the hall, his face inches apart from hers. Rae locked her arms around his shoulders and easily matched her steps to his. No, it wasn't even like she was trying to match him. When they were RaeAnthony, her body and his body moved together perfectly, like they were two halves that had been rejoined as soon as Rae and Anthony kissed.

They made it out of the school and through the parking lot to Anthony's Hyundai, still holding on to each other. Anthony backed Rae up against the passenger side door, then slowly, reluctantly let go of her with one arm to slide his hand into his pocket. Rae heard the jangle of keys; then she felt Anthony fumbling to unlock the door behind her. *Wonder how many times I can make him drop them today?* she thought. She eased away from him, just the tiniest bit, then smiled and leaned in to kiss him again.

And the keys hit the asphalt. Rae loved that she could do that to Anthony—make him tremble so bad, he couldn't keep his grip on a set of keys. Of course, he could do it right back to her, which she loved just about as much.

Anthony bent her back at the waist—like a tango dancer—as he reached to retrieve the keys. There wasn't a fraction of an inch of space between their bodies. Rae opened her eyes, needing to look at Anthony. His eyes, his melted-Hershey's-Kiss brown eyes, opened a second later. It was like that with them. They were so in sync. RaeAnthony. AnthonyRae.

"Got 'em," Anthony said, his lips sliding off hers and onto her cheek. He straightened up, pulling Rae with him.

"Anthony," she gasped.

He gave her a shy smile, about to lean in for another kiss.

"No, Anthony," Rae blurted out as she tightened her hands on his shoulders. She could feel her nails starting to dig into his skin, but she couldn't loosen her grip. "There's someone in the backseat of the car," she said, a familiar waver entering her voice. One week. She'd gotten one week free of fear, and now it was all rushing back. "On the floor," she managed to get out.

Anthony jerked his head toward the back window, already pushing Rae behind him to make his body a kind of shield for her. Rae held her breath, and then Anthony looked back at her, reassurance in his eyes. "It's Aiden," he told her.

Rae let out a shaky sigh of relief. Aiden Matthews had saved her life more than once. If that didn't mean she could trust him, what did? Anthony unlocked Rae's door, and she climbed in. "Don't look at me," Aiden ordered. He repeated the instruction when Anthony got behind the wheel. "Just drive," he continued. "Not fast. It should look like the two of you are just off to the mall or wherever it is you go."

"What's wrong?" Anthony demanded as he pulled out of the parking space and headed out of the lot.

"Yana escaped," Aiden answered.

Rae felt like her blood had been replaced by novocaine. Her body went all thick and heavy . . . and dead. "Yana," she whispered, her tongue stumbling over the name.

Anthony reached over and grabbed her hand. She could barely feel the warmth and strength of his fingers. "Nothing's going to happen to you," he said fiercely.

Rae flashed on the cabin, the cabin where Yana—Yana, who had been her very best friend less than a month ago—had taken Rae to kill her. Rae saw herself holding a knife, being forced by Yana's thought-implanting ability to run it across her throat, lightly, lightly. Yana had wanted Rae to die slowly. She'd wanted to watch Rae suffer. And now Yana was out there somewhere. And what else would she be doing but coming after Rae, wanting to make sure Rae ended up dead this time?

"Did you tell Yana the truth?" Anthony asked, glaring at the road in front of him. He jerked the car to a stop at a red light. "Did you tell her that Rae's mom didn't kill her mother? Did you tell her that it's your friggin' secret government agency she should be going after?"

"It was never *my* agency. And I'm not a part of it anymore," Aiden answered.

"Did you tell her?" Anthony insisted, pulling across the intersection.

Rae tried to tighten her grip on Anthony's hand, but she was too numb, frozen all the way to her bones.

"I tried," Aiden said.

"What does that mean?" Anthony shot back.

"It means I tried," Aiden answered, a slight edge to his voice. "I explained it all, but I don't know how much she understood. I had to keep her heavily sedated so she wouldn't be able to use her power, so she was only semiconscious. But I told her that the agency killed her mother because her mother was going to expose them for the experiments they'd done on her and the other women in the group. The experiments that gave Rae's mother and Yana's mother their powers."

"That ended up mutating Rae and Yana, too. Don't forget that side effect of the experiments," Anthony reminded him.

"Did she . . . ?" Anthony and Aiden waited while Rae struggled to get the words out of her deadened mouth. "Did she believe you? About my mom?"

There was a long silence from the back of the car. "I don't know," Aiden finally admitted. "I planned to explain everything to her again when I thought it was safe to lower the doses of her drugs. But—"

"But she escaped," Anthony interrupted. "How in the hell did that happen?"

"There was a power surge. It messed up the security system on the doors to her room—the locks opened when they weren't supposed to," Aiden explained. "She got out the back while I was trying to get the system running again."

"She could be in Atlanta already," Rae said. "You are. So she could be." She turned her head, the cold muscles in her neck almost creaking, and stared out at the people on the sidewalk closest to the car. No Yana. Not yet.

"She didn't have any money or—" Aiden began.

"Are you insane?" Anthony burst out. "She doesn't need money. She can inject thoughts into people's heads."

"Let's just figure out how we can find her," Rae said, eyes still searching the sidewalk. "Before she finds me."

"We don't know that she's coming for you," Aiden answered.

She is, though, Rae thought. *I can feel her out there. Coming closer.*

"Where exactly were you keeping her?" Anthony

demanded. "How far out of town? We need to retrace her steps."

"I can't tell you that. I can't tell you anything more. I shouldn't even be talking to you now," Aiden said. "If they knew—"

"So you don't care if they kill me?" Rae asked, the novocaine in her veins heating up, turning to acid.

"Of course I care. That's why I'm here. To warn you," Aiden protested. Rae wished she could see his face. She wished she could make him look into her eyes while he pretended to care so much. But he was still crouched on the floor of the backseat.

"And that's it? A warning? That's all you plan to freakin' do?" Anthony exploded. He answered his own question before Aiden could. "There's no way that's happening. You are not getting out of this car until we find Yana."

"Red light," Rae warned Anthony. "Red light!"

Anthony slammed on the brakes. The back door swung open, and Aiden scrambled out into the street. He zigzagged across the lane of oncoming traffic.

"He's gone," Rae said, watching Aiden disappear around a corner.

"Bastard," Anthony muttered. He squeezed Rae's hand so hard, she felt the small bones rub together. "Don't worry," he said. "We don't need him to find Yana."

Maybe we shouldn't be trying to find her, Rae thought. *Maybe it's a mistake, a huge mistake where RaeAnthony ends up dead.*

Yana Savari stopped at the red light. "Red means stop. Green means go," she muttered. Like on the door. Green. So go.

"Do you need help crossing the street?" a voice asked. "You can cross with me."

"Are you . . . me?" Yana replied, turning toward the voice and peering down at the striped blobby thing that stood next to her. "Are you . . . me?" she repeated when the blobby didn't answer. The words . . . not right. The right ones . . . stuck in the sticky stuff inside her brain.

"I can go get my mommy," the blobby said. Why could Yana understand the blobby words but not make the right words herself? She gave a little growl of frustration, and the blobby backed away. Then the light turned green.

Green, go. Like the door. In the room. Red, red, red, red. Watching, watching. Red, red, red. Then green. Green for go. Like now. Green light. Yana bolted across the street, leaving the blobby behind her. Go, go, go. Something red. Over there. She hesitated, peering at it. No. Not a light. Don't stop. Go, go, go. Run, run, run.

Red. Red light. Means stop. Means door locked. Can't get out. Red light. Yana stopped next to the yellow-and-blue blobby. Not as blobby as the other one. More . . . hard? Solid. More solid. Yana rubbed her eyes. More, more solid. A person. A . . . um . . . what? A . . . a man person. Yellow shirt. Blue jeans.

"Are you okay?" the man asked.

Yana's forehead crinkled as she tried to find the word in her sticky head. She got it, then pushed it out of her mouth. "Yes," she answered.

"You sure?" the man asked.

"Yes." The word came out more easily. Then suddenly there were words everywhere, bouncing around in her head, unstuck. They came spilling out of her mouth. "My mother. My mother. She's dead. Murdered. Someone's got to pay."

Anthony took a slug of his massive coffee. He'd gotten the guy at the 7-Eleven to fill up a Big Gulp cup because he'd known he was in for a long night and he wanted to be wide awake for every second of it.

Is Rae awake, too? he wondered, staring through his recently Windexed windshield at her bedroom window. *Is she lying there terrified that any second Yana's going to show?* He wished he could tell her he was out here, watching. But if he did, she'd probably insist he go home. And that wasn't going to happen.

"Come on, Yana, where are you?" Anthony muttered. He had to see her before she saw him—or his hands could be the ones that ended up killing Rae. That night in the cabin, when Yana had taken control of his mind and started to make him feed Rae rat poison, that had been the worst night of his life. For three nights afterward he'd had a dream where Aiden hadn't brought Yana down with the tranquilizer gun, where Anthony had kept Rae's mouth pried open and shoveled the poison down her throat until she foamed out of the mouth and convulsed over and over. Then Anthony'd woken up screaming. And yeah, with snot and freakin' tears on his pillow.

Just thinking about the dream had him pumping sweat. *All you have to do is make sure that you see her first,* he told himself again. *You gotta take her down before she has a chance to claw her way into your head.*

Anthony took another gulp of the coffee. His eyes were burning, but he forced himself to scan Rae's front yard, then check up and down the street. Nothing. So far. He rubbed his eyes with the heels of his hands, then returned his attention to Rae's yard.

Crap, he'd rubbed too hard. There were all these little squiggles of red running across his vision. He blinked rapidly, then peered out at the yard again.

His heart kicked into his ribs. Someone was out

there. A girl. Moving toward Rae's window. Yana. Had to be.

Anthony eased open the car door and slowly climbed out of the Hyundai. Had she heard him? *If she had, she'd already have taken you over,* Anthony told himself. He pulled out the stun gun he'd bought off one of the guys who hung around the 7-Eleven parking lot, then crouched down, locked his gaze on Yana, and hurled himself across the street and over the grass.

He got Yana just behind the knees. She went down hard. But the stun gun flew out of Anthony's hand, landing halfway across the lawn. She had him. She totally had him now. She'd be in his head before he twitched a finger.

Rae's eyelids snapped open. There was someone outside her window. *It's probably just that calico cat,* she told herself as she slipped out of bed. *Or Yana,* she couldn't stop herself from adding.

Cat. Yana. Cat. Yana. The words thudded through her head as she crept up to the window. She pulled the curtain aside an inch and peeked outside.

Mandy Reese smiled at her and gave an apologetic wave. Rae's heart rate returned to normal, and she began to slide the window up, then caught a flash of motion in the darkness. Before she could move, before she could shout a warning, Mandy was thrown to the ground.

By Anthony. 'Cause that's who had come racing across her front lawn. Anthony. He had his knee on Mandy's back, and he was straining to reach . . . a stun gun!

Rae jerked the window all the way up. "Anthony, no!" she cried. "It's Mandy. It's *Mandy.*"

Instantly Anthony jerked his knee off Mandy's back. He stood up and gently helped her to her feet. "Are you okay?" he asked. "I thought you were Yana."

"Yana?" Mandy exclaimed, fear giving her voice a jagged edge. "Why would Yana—"

"You guys have to be quiet. We don't want to wake up my dad," Rae cautioned them. "Go to the front door. I'll let you in." Without waiting for an answer, Rae quickly threw on the jeans and shirt she'd been wearing earlier, then hurried out of her bedroom and down the stairs. She turned the lock on the front door slowly, but it still made a click that sounded as loud as a gunshot to Rae's ears. She hesitated a moment, listening. But she didn't hear any movement from her dad's room, so she swung open the door, gestured Anthony and Mandy inside, and led them back into her room.

"Are you okay?" she asked Mandy as soon as she'd shut the door behind them.

"Yeah. I'm fine," she said, speaking half to Rae and half to Anthony. "But what's the deal with Yana? I thought Aiden had her locked away, loaded with drugs."

"She escaped," Anthony answered.

"God. Oh God." Mandy sat down on the edge of Rae's bed.

"You're safe," Anthony told her. "Yana's got no reason to be coming after you. She probably didn't even see you that night in the cabin, and there's no way she knows that you used your power to help track her down."

"I'm not worried about that," Mandy said. She turned to Rae. "But I should be asking if you're okay, not the other way around. What she tried to do to you at the cabin—" Mandy shook her head as if she couldn't stand to even think about it.

"I'm okay, really," Rae told her. It was a lie, but she wanted to keep Mandy out of this. Mandy'd done enough for Rae already. Her mother had been in the same group that Rae's mother and Yana's mother had been in. And Mandy's genes had been screwed up by the experiments that had been done on her mom, just the way Rae's and Yana's had been screwed up.

But Mandy hadn't known that until Yana had taken Rae hostage. Then Aiden and Anthony had told Mandy the truth about herself. They'd told Mandy that she had some kind of psychic ability that would start showing itself when she was at the height of puberty. They said that they thought her power—whatever it was—might help them save Rae. So Mandy, even though she barely knew Rae, had agreed to let Aiden give her an injection of hormones to bring out her power right away. And it was some power, too—it turned out that Mandy could touch an item of clothing belonging to someone and "see" that person. Actually, more like *be* the person for a few minutes. She'd used Rae's sweater to figure out where Yana'd taken Rae.

"Why don't I believe you?" Mandy asked Rae.

"Because you're a smart girl," Anthony muttered.

"Why were you even over here tonight?" Rae asked, not wanting to drag Mandy deeper into Rae's personal nightmare. The girl was only fourteen. She should be out doing . . . fun stuff. Normal stuff.

Mandy started making a little braid in her long, light brown hair. "It's stupid. I'm sorry. I shouldn't have come running over here so late."

"Bathroom," Anthony mouthed at Rae, then quietly left her and Mandy alone.

"It's not stupid," Rae said as she sat down next to Mandy. "When I found out I could get thoughts from fingerprints, I completely freaked. Are you freaking about your powers?"

"Yeah," Mandy admitted. "Plus that hormone shot did something to my breasts. I wanted them to be bigger, but they've been growing so fast, they ache."

Rae winced. "Ouch. Mandy, you know how sorry—"

"Oh, shut up," Mandy interrupted. "I told you I don't want you to apologize. Anyway, that's not why I came over."

Rae picked up one of the dark green pillows off the head of her bed and cradled it to her chest. "So what is going on?"

Anthony came back in and hesitated. He raised an eyebrow at Rae. "Is it okay if Anthony's here?" she asked Mandy.

"Sure. But like I said, it's nothing that I needed to talk to you about in the middle of the night. Not with the Yana thing happening," Mandy said.

"We both owe you," Anthony told her as he sat down in Rae's black leather desk chair. "If you have a problem, we want to help."

Do I have a great guy or what? Rae thought before she turned her full attention back to Mandy.

"My sister, Emma? She's always been sickeningly good. She always does her homework right away. She tutors these kids at the elementary school. God, she irons her jeans," Mandy said. "At least that's how she used to be. But since my mom died . . . was murdered . . ." Mandy corrected herself. She paused, her eyes glazing over. "I can still hardly believe that crazy scientist guy killed her," she murmured.

Rae knew exactly how Mandy felt. Steve Mercer, the man who'd shocked and drugged and radiated her mother—and Yana's and Mandy's—had murdered Rae's mother, too. He'd gone crazy and killed the members of the group he thought were dangerous to society. He would have killed Rae if the agency that funded the experiments—the agency where Aiden used to work—hadn't killed him first. It was so eerie knowing that somebody had actually gone after her mother like that, and she could only imagine how much scarier it would be for Mandy, since she'd already been a teenager when it happened. Rae had only been a baby when her mother died.

"So, your sister," Anthony prodded gently.

Mandy gave her head a little shake. "Right," she said. "I touched this shirt of hers, and I *was* her, you know?" Rae and Anthony nodded. "And I . . . she was making out with this gross guy, Zeke. She never would have even spoken to scum like him when Mom was alive. And I could tell . . . I could *feel* how into him she is. He's going to hurt her. I know it. But there's no way she's going to listen to her stupid baby sister about something like that."

"Maybe he's not as bad as he seems," Anthony said, using his feet to turn the chair back and forth and back and forth. "What makes you think he's scum?" He gave an extra-hard shove with his feet and spun the chair completely around.

"How about the fact that he's stoned pretty much every second of the day?" Mandy answered. "I think he might even be dealing a little. What if Emma starts doing that crap, too? She practically has this scholarship to UCLA in the bag, but she's going to totally screw it up if she keeps hanging with Zeke."

Mandy started wrapping her little braid around her finger. Rae'd seen her do that before when she was stressed. God, she practically pulled the hair out of her head.

"Look, tomorrow's Saturday. How about if I help you check out this Zeke guy?" Rae said. She gently pulled the little braid out of Mandy's fingers.

"Don't you think we should be—" Anthony began.

Rae shook her head. "I think we should just do what we'd usually do, 'cause what other choice do we have?" She smiled at Mandy. "And what I'd usually be doing is trying to get a scum-reading on your sister's guy."

"Thanks," Mandy said. "I . . . just thanks." She

turned back to Anthony. "But you were going to say something about looking for Yana, right?"

Anthony glanced at Rae, then slowly nodded.

"You're right," Mandy told him. "We have to help my sister, but we have to find Yana first. So what do we do?"

Rae tilted her head to the side. Mandy sounded so much like Rae and Anthony's friend Jesse. Eager to help, ready to throw herself into something extremely dangerous for Rae's sake. In the middle of all the horrible stuff that had happened to Rae recently, she'd made some pretty amazing friends.

Anthony coughed. "That's basically the problem," he said. "We don't know what to do. We have no idea where Yana could be right now." He shrugged. "So we just have to wait," he said, his voice tightening on the last word.

Mandy narrowed her eyes in concentration. "Maybe not," she said. "Maybe there *is* something we can do. Well, something *I* can do."

Rae frowned. "Mandy, I don't want you—"

"No, she's right," Anthony said, his eyes taking on an excited gleam. "And don't worry, Rae, she won't be in any danger."

What was Rae missing here? She stared at both of them, then finally got it.

"Your power," she blurted.

"Yes," Mandy said. "Anthony, can you get me something of Yana's? Something she's worn?"

"Definitely," Anthony answered. "I'll bring it to you tomorrow. And once we know where Yana is, we go after her."

God, Rae thought, shivering. *Am I going to end up bringing them both into something none of us will survive?*

Chapter 2

Someone was watching her. She could feel hot snail-trails crisscrossing her body where their eyes touched her.

Yana cracked open her eyelids and did a survey of her surroundings. Yeah. Uh-huh. Skeevy guy at four o'clock leering at her and thinking—she didn't even want to know what. If she did, she'd have to soap out her brain. *Well, what'd you expect, sleeping in a bus station?* she asked herself.

She stood up slowly, her vertebrae cracking. *Note to self,* she thought. *Sleeping on a wooden bench sucks.* At least the drugs Aiden had pumped into her had worn off. Yana lightly fingered the bruise on the inside of her left arm. It formed a circle around the red pinprick where the needle had gone in. A few hours ago she could have been deep in conversation with a poodle or a trash can and thought it was her best friend. That's how messed up she'd been.

Yana shot the skeev a dirty look, then headed over to the bathroom. She could see the little triangle-skirted woman on the door nice and clear, luckily. This wasn't a place where you wanted to wander into the wrong john. She stepped inside, went straight to the closest sink, and splashed her face with cold water. Aaah! Even better. She was getting focused now. Getting sharp. She looked like hell—her bloodshot blue eyes were like some hideous Fourth of July decoration, and her skin was a sickly yellowish color. But in her head she was getting close to a hundred percent. Okay, that was bull. But she was past the fifty percent mark and moving up. Her next step was clear.

Yana looked around for some paper towels to dry her face. The place only had an air dryer. She stepped in front of it, cranked the fat nozzle up, and punched the button. With a roar, hot air hit her face. It actually felt kind of good. Anything real felt good after the drug haze she'd been in when she'd broken out of the observation room Aiden had locked her in. Make that walked out when the security system crashed. The shape she'd been in, she wouldn't have been able to break out of a plastic bag.

When the dryer kicked off, Yana combed her white-blond hair with her fingers, then headed out of the bathroom. She hurried directly to the ticket booth. *Okay, let's see if I've still got it,* she thought. She smiled at the woman behind the counter. "I'll take a one-way to Atlanta," she said. Then she reached into her pocket and pulled out a Big Red gum wrapper.

THAT'S A FIFTY. She imagined throwing the thought at the woman—like a softball to the forehead. Would it work? Or had whatever crap Aiden had given her somehow spayed her?

Yana's smile widened as the woman put the gum wrapper under the drawer of her cash register—where the big bills went—and then started counting out the change.

By the time I get back to Atlanta, I'll be at a hundred percent, she promised herself as the woman handed her her ticket and change. *And I'll be ready to do what needs to be done.* "For you, Mom," she whispered.

"Okay, so right arm, turn head to left, left arm, turn head to right," Rae said. "Anthony, hello, are you listening?"

"Right arm, head left, yep," he answered. He'd gotten so caught up in looking at her, her wet hair curling around her face, droplets of water shining on her shoulders, her bathing suit—

Rae stepped closer to him, moving through the half chlorine, half water of the Y pool. "What are you thinking about? Because it's definitely not my swimming lesson." She smiled, and her smile made him think that she knew exactly what he was thinking. And that she liked it. Which was so friggin' mind-blowing.

"Come on, tell me." She looped her arms around his neck, and the old lady getting ready to swim laps gave them an "awww" kind of look.

"I was thinking that you look good in that suit," Anthony answered. He was pretty sure he'd choke if he tried to say any of the other stuff.

"Oh, really? I—" Rae whipped her head to the left.

"What?" Anthony demanded, scanning the area around the pool.

"Nothing," Rae answered, sliding her arms off his neck. "I just, God, I thought I saw Yana. But it was only that woman in the white bathing cap. She doesn't even look like her."

Anthony checked the big clock behind the diving board. "I should be able to head over to Yana's in about half an hour. Her dad'll be up and functioning by then—even on a Saturday. You'll feel better when we can do something to find Yana."

"Yeah. Yeah, you're right," Rae said. But she didn't sound convinced. "Let's get out, okay? I'm freezing in here."

Anthony was pretty sure the temperature of the water had nothing to do with the shivers ripping through Rae. But he didn't call her on it. He just followed her up the stairs in the shallow end and over to the deck chairs they'd staked out. Rae grabbed a towel, leaned forward, and started drying her hair. "Wonder what I'd be like if I'd grown up thinking my mom was murdered. Instead of a murder*er*. I mean, I could totally have turned out like Yana."

"What?" Anthony demanded. He'd couldn't freakin' believe her. "What?" he repeated. He reached out, caught her chin in his fingers, and gently raised her head until she was looking him in the eye. "Do you actually think that you'd have tried to kill someone if you thought your mom had been killed?"

Rae bit her lip. "I wanted to kill Steve Mercer when I found out that he murdered my mom," she answered. "If I'd known that my whole life, I'd probably have wanted to kill him a million times more."

"Fine. I get that. And I'd probably even have helped you if the agency hadn't taken him out. But let me ask you this. Now that Mercer's dead, do you feel, like, any desire to find out if he had a kid and then kill the kid?"

"God, of course not!" Rae exclaimed.

"Well, that's exactly what Yana did," Anthony reminded her, struggling to keep his anger in check. "She thought your mom killed her mom. But your mom was dead, so, Yana decided, 'What the hell—I'll just kill the daughter. That'll make me happy.' "

"Yeah, yeah, you're right," Rae answered. "It's just . . ." She let her words trail off and started rubbing the drops of water off her arms. Rubbing so hard, it was like she wanted to take off a layer of skin, too.

"It's just what?" Anthony pressed.

"I don't know—she brought me doughnuts on my first day back at school because she knew how horrible it was going to be for me," Rae mumbled.

"So we got doughnuts on one side." Anthony stuck out his left hand. "And on the other side—" He stuck out his right hand. "We got Yana trying to *kill* you." He moved his hands up and down, pretending to weigh both sides.

"I get it," Rae told him.

Anthony dropped his hands to his sides. "Do you? 'Cause if you don't, you're not going to be careful enough." He didn't want to freak her out. Wait. Yeah, he did. If that's what it took to make sure she kept herself safe, then that's what he wanted. "Right now Yana's out there coming up with another plan to make you dead."

"I know. I get it. All right? I get it," Rae snapped. She wrapped her towel around her shoulders. "I'm going to go change."

"I'll meet you right outside the locker-room door," Anthony promised.

"You sure you don't want to come in and watch me change?" Rae shot back.

"Is that an offer?" Anthony joked, his imagination already going there.

Rae smiled. "Sorry, but no."

"I wasn't trying to piss you off before," Anthony said. "I know you can handle yourself. I just . . . worry."

"Yeah. Me too," Rae admitted.

"Last night I had a dream about Steve Mercer," Mandy confessed. She pulled an old sweatshirt out from under her pillow. Rae recognized the sweatshirt—it had belonged to Mandy's mom. "I don't even know what the guy looks like, but in the dream I knew it was him. And I was some kind of superhero, but a sort of evil one. Like Catwoman, but without the skintight outfit. Anyway. I hurled Mercer onto the ground, and I stomped on him over and over. Until blood started to leak out of his ears." Mandy used both hands to push her long, light brown hair away from her face. "Very nice, huh?"

"Very normal," Rae answered, thinking about the conversation she'd just had with Anthony at the pool.

"So there's not, like, a psycho killer inside me, ready to pop out?" Mandy asked, without meeting Rae's eyes.

"If there's one in you, there's one in me. 'Cause I've definitely had some nasty fantasies about torturing Mercer," Rae told her. "I . . . I know that you and Yana and I have a lot in common. Moms who were murdered because of the group. Genes that have been messed with. But that doesn't mean the two of us are going to turn out like Yana."

Mandy held the sweatshirt up to her face, pulled in a deep breath, then tucked the sweatshirt back under her pillow. "She seemed so cool that time she was over here with you. She seemed to really get how I was feeling about my mom's death and everything."

"I know. I felt the same way. When I thought I was going nuts—before I knew I had my fingerprint thing—Yana was . . ." Rae hesitated, flashing on the conversation with Anthony. He wouldn't like to hear what she was about to say, but she said it, anyway. "Yana kept me going. I might have lost it completely if it wasn't for her."

"But it was all a big lie, right? From the beginning, she was out to get you," Mandy said.

"Yeah. I'm sure getting herself assigned as a volunteer in the mental hospital was even part of her plan," Rae answered. Except Yana had been so decent to—

Stop. When are you going to accept that Yana completely played you? Rae asked herself. *Why are you still trying to believe that some of your so-called friendship was actually real?*

"Anthony'll probably show up soon with something of Yana's. You want to give me some of your sister's boyfriend's stuff to touch before he gets here?" Rae asked, going for a screeching subject change.

"That would be so great. I've got a whole collection of Zeke skankobilia," Mandy answered. She jumped off the bed and picked up a shoe box off the floor, kicking an empty Ben & Jerry's container out of the way. "Here you go." She dropped the box next to Rae.

Rae pulled a Kleenex out of her purse and wiped the coat of wax off the fingers of her right hand so she'd be ready to receive fingerprint info. "Here goes," she muttered. She picked up a Howard Stern coffee mug with her left hand and then ran the unprotected fingers of her right over the mug's slick ceramic surface.

/wearing panties?/bitter/what was/dad home?/to couch/

Rae set the mug down. The taste of overbrewed coffee filled her mouth. And God, she felt . . . horny. That was the only word for it. Like she'd just spent an hour kissing Anthony and—

"Well?" Mandy snapped her fingers in front of Rae's face. Then she stared at her hand as if her fingers had snapped by themselves. "Sorry. Man, that was rude. But what'd you get?"

"Uhhh." Rae didn't want to tell Mandy that Zeke was thinking about whether or not her dad was home—probably because he wanted to find out if Mandy's sister was wearing panties. "Let me try something else."

Rae pulled the empty Doritos bag out of the shoe box and did a fingerprint sweep.

/front clasp?/Dorito gunk/my house/the zipper/get it/

I'm surprised that I'm not setting off the smoke detector, Rae thought. Her breath was actually coming in fast pants.

"What?" Mandy demanded. "It's something bad, isn't it?"

"No," Rae assured her. "He has sex on the brain. But he's a guy. I mean, most guys Emma goes out with probably think about sex a ton."

"That's it? Nothing about dealing? Nothing about being high whenever he's not asleep?" Mandy asked, her voice getting higher and higher.

Rae shook her head. "Not yet, anyway. I'll keep going." She took a pen—one of those big fat ones that write in twenty colors—out of the box.

"Oh, wait, that's Emma's," Mandy said. Her voice sounded far away, almost lost under the rush of not-Rae thoughts.

/his name?/daisies/no church/ballistic/married/

Rae gave the pen a half turn and moved her fingers over the new area. Her hands trembled with an excitement that wasn't hers.

/elope/white eyelet/why graduate?/Zeke can/soon/soon/no finals/

Mandy pulled the pen out of Rae's shaking hands. "It wasn't just about sex this time, was it?" she asked softly.

Rae tried not to smile. This was serious. But Emma's happiness was making her giddy. "It seems like . . . Mandy, I'm pretty sure Emma wants to drop out of school."

"What?" Mandy cried. "That's insane. I told you she's been killing herself for that scholarship." Mandy dumped the cardboard box onto the floor. "It's because of Zeke. I'm right, aren't I? It's his fault."

"Sort of," Rae admitted. "I think—I think Emma's considering eloping with him."

Chapter 3

I've barely even been in Yana's house, Anthony realized as he started up the front walk. And she'd only been to his house once or twice. They'd spent most of their time in one of their cars, usually making out.

Anthony grimaced. Thinking about kissing Yana was like bad food repeating on him, bringing up a sour, rotten taste. How could he have been such a freakin' moron? Yana had completely—

The front door swung open, yanking Anthony away from his thoughts. "You got the wrong house," Yana's dad barked, clearly not recognizing Anthony. His sandy brown hair was sticking up, and his eyes were half glued shut with eye gunk. He must have just rolled out of the sack.

Good morning to you, too, jerk, Anthony thought. "I'm a friend of Yana's," he reminded him. The lie brought up the spoiled food taste again. He swallowed hard and kept going. "She borrowed some English notes from me, and I need to get them back. Is she around?"

"No, she's—who the hell knows where she is," Yana's dad answered. He hitched up his sweats. "But I can tell you this, she's not going to be happy once she finally decides to show up."

He didn't actually sound like he gave a crap. Not that it would be so different at Anthony's place if Anthony went missing for a few days. No, that wasn't true. If Anthony pulled a disappearing act, the rug rats would be screaming because there was nothing to eat and no one to referee the fights over the remote. His mother and Tom would actually have to act like parents for once. So they'd be wanting him back. His mom would probably even get all teary. She still called him her baby sometimes, even though he was seventeen.

"Doodles, where'd you go?" a woman called from the back of the house.

"Be right there," Yana's father called back.

Guess that's why he didn't seem so worried, Anthony thought, trying not to cringe. *He's having a little sleepover while his kid is, as he said, who the hell knows where.* Yana's dad started to swing the door shut. "Wait. I really need those notes," Anthony said quickly. "Can I look in her backpack? It'll only take a minute." He wasn't leaving without a piece of Yana's clothing. He was tracking the girl down today.

"One minute," Yana's dad said. "Shut the door on your way out." He disappeared back into the house. Anthony followed him inside through the living room and down the hall. Yana's dad went in the room at the end of the hall and shut the door behind him.

Didn't even bother to ask if I'd seen her around or knew anyplace she might be, Anthony thought as he followed Yana's father inside. The guy rivaled Tom. And he was actually Yana's blood relative, too. *Yana must—*

"Man, are you actually feeling sorry for her?" Anthony muttered, disgusted with himself. *So her dad doesn't treat her like a princess. Boo freakin' hoo. That's no excuse. There is no excuse for what Yana did to Rae.*

There were two doors off the hall besides the one Yana's dad had gone in. Anthony tried the closest one. He would have thought it belonged to Yana's little sister—except he knew Yana didn't have a little sister. There was a pink plaid bedspread on the single bed. A row of worn stuffed animals was propped neatly against the ruffly pillow. Who would have thought tough-girl Yana would still have stuffed animals? Maybe she wasn't as tough as—

Do you have fried eggs for brains or what? Anthony asked himself. *The girl is a killer. Or she would be if she'd gotten even a little bit luckier. The fact that she sleeps with Winnie the friggin' Pooh doesn't change that. Now do what you've got to do and get out of here.*

Anthony scanned the room, looking for a shirt tossed over a chair, a pair of jeans balled up in the corner. But nothing. He yanked open the flimsy double doors of Yana's closet. Her clothes were all on hangers. No laundry bag of dirty clothes in sight. Anthony wasn't sure if Mandy needed clothes that had been worn recently or not. He turned around and jerked open the top dresser drawer. The socks and underwear inside were way too neatly arranged to have been worn. The clothes in the next two drawers were clean, too. Anthony grabbed a T-shirt, then slammed the dresser drawers shut and closed the closet. Not that Yana's dad would care.

On the way out he swung into the bathroom and checked the hamper. A bunch of Yana's dad's clothes, but nothing of Yana's. He found a mini washer and dryer in the kitchen, but no clothes.

Forget it. The T-shirt was good enough. It would have to be.

"What if she's pregnant?" Mandy asked as she paced back and forth in front of the bed. "That has to be why she wants to elope, right? This is a disaster. My dad's going to stroke out. He's still all"—Mandy circled her hands helplessly—"because of my mom and—" The doorbell interrupted her.

"It's probably Anthony. Want me to get it?" Rae asked.

"Yeah. Would you?" Mandy answered. "I just—"

Rae stood up and gently steered Mandy onto the bed. "Sit. I'll be right back." She hurried to the front door and opened it.

"Did you check the peephole first?" Anthony demanded.

"I knew it was you," Rae told him.

"You didn't know it was me. You *thought* it was me," he shot back, his deep brown eyes getting even darker. "It could have been Yana. In three seconds she could have had you scarfing down Drano."

Before Anthony could continue lecturing her, Rae leaned up and wrapped her arms around his neck, pulling his face closer to hers. The second their lips touched, the kiss took over Rae's whole body. She could feel the warmth on her neck, on her knees, on her toes. It was like he could somehow kiss every part of her without moving his mouth from hers.

"Next time check the peephole," he said when he released her.

Rae nodded. She didn't think she could speak. Not so soon after that kiss. She led the way down the hall and into Mandy's room.

"Did you get me something?" Mandy asked the second she saw Anthony. He pulled a T-shirt with the words Boys Lie printed across the front and tossed it to her. Mandy bunched the material in both fists and closed her eyes. Her forehead got all crinkly. She squeezed her eyes shut more tightly. Rae could see the tension spread from the muscles of her face to her neck and shoulders.

"Anything?" Anthony finally asked.

Mandy opened her eyes and shook her head. "I'm sorry. I don't know why. I just—there was nothing."

"Crap," Anthony spat out. Rae shot him a be-sensitive look. He got the message. "I was afraid that might happen," he told Mandy. "I couldn't find any dirty stuff. I mean stuff that Yana had worn but hadn't washed yet. You need something that hasn't been through the wash, don't you?"

"I don't know," Mandy admitted. "I haven't been

experimenting with my, uh, thing too much. It kind of freaks me out," she added, sounding apologetic. "But the sweater I touched of my sister's wasn't something right out of the wash, so maybe . . ."

Mandy stood up. "Come on." She led the way to her sister's bedroom. The place still freaked Rae out. It was like a temple or something, with all these pictures of Mandy and Emma's mom everywhere, each picture with dried flowers or a little candle next to it. Rae could completely get Emma missing her mom, grieving, having that empty hole-in-the-chest feeling. But didn't it make it worse being surrounded with the pictures? God, in the spaces where there weren't pictures or flowers or candles, there were things that had belonged to Mandy and Emma's mom—jewelry and purses. Even her driver's license.

"Maybe you're right," Mandy said to Anthony. Rae jerked her attention away from the objects in the room and realized Mandy was holding a silk blouse. "Emma just got this back from the dry cleaners', and it gave me nothing." Mandy tossed the blouse onto Emma's bed, then pulled a bra out of her sister's dresser.

Rae took a quick glance at Anthony out of the corner of her eye. It felt weird having him checking out some other girl's underwear. Not that he was checking the bra out, exactly. But he was looking at it.

"Nothing from this, either. But it's clean, too," Mandy announced. She shoved the bra back in the drawer. "Let me try one more thing." She pulled back the bedspread on her sister's bed, reached under the pillow, and pulled out a pajama top. Immediately her head began to sway back and forth. Her hips, too. A smile tugged at her lips, but she wasn't smiling at Rae or Anthony. Her eyes were blank and vacant.

Rae took a half step closer to Anthony, and he looped his arm around her shoulders. They watched Mandy in silence for five or six seconds. Then Mandy's body gave a spasm, she blinked, and Rae could tell she was back in the room, back from wherever it was she'd been.

"I guess the washed or not-washed thing is what makes the difference," Mandy said, letting the pajama top drop back onto the bed. "I saw her that time."

"So we're screwed," Anthony answered. "I couldn't find anything of Yana's that hadn't been washed."

Rae felt something shift inside her, but she wasn't sure if it was disappointment or relief. "What'd you see, Mandy?" she asked, remembering that Mandy needed her right now.

Mandy shook her head. "It was crazy—for a few seconds I *was* my sister. It's like I was right in her skin. She was hanging out at the Virgin Megastore with Zeke. They were sharing a set of headphones, listening to some Afroman song."

"That doesn't sound so terrible," Anthony commented.

"I got some fingerprint info before," Rae explained softly. "It looks like Mandy's sister might drop out of school and elope with the guy."

"Huh," Anthony muttered. "That's not so good."

Rae turned her attention to Mandy. "We shouldn't get all ahead of ourselves. Emma was thinking about eloping, yeah. But everybody thinks about stuff they don't actually do." *Except thinking about marrying Zeke made her so happy,* Rae couldn't help adding inwardly.

"I guess so," Mandy agreed. "Do you think if you went fingertip-to-fingertip with Zeke, you could find out more? Maybe Emma's a lot more serious about him than he is about her. Maybe he would go nuts if he thought she wanted to elope."

Mandy looked at Rae with full-on puppy-dog eyes. Full-on *worried* puppy-dog eyes. So what choice did Rae have? "I guess we could stop by Virgin," Rae told her. "I could use some new CDs." She ran one finger down Anthony's back. "What do you say?"

"You two go ahead," he answered. "I'm gonna see if I can locate our friend Aiden."

"How?" Rae asked. "We don't know where he's living now. We don't even know where he was keeping Yana."

"You need help?" Mandy asked, even though Rae knew she was dying to deal with her sister's sitch.

"No. I've got it covered. And besides, you two wouldn't be able to get in the places I need to go. Not with your baby faces." Anthony's tone was teasing, but his hands were starting to ball into fists—a sure sign that he was stressing.

"Are you sure you—" Rae began.

"I'll be fine," he cut her off. "You're the one who needs to be careful. Did you ever hang with Yana at Virgin?"

Rae shook her head.

"Good," Anthony said. "You'll be safer there than anyplace you've been with her, places she'd think to look for you. I'll call you on your cell every hour and check in." He slowly slid his arm away from Rae's shoulders, and she felt a chill settle into her body. For a few minutes she'd actually forgotten that Yana could be anywhere.

Even though that's not exactly true, Rae thought. *Or not the whole truth, anyway. Yes, Yana* could *be anywhere right now. But admit it, wherever she is, you know that she's moving closer to you.*

"You again."

Mr. Pink—yeah, he had on a pink shirt again—had only said two words, and already Anthony was feeling like a five-year-old who had peed in his Batman Underoos. What was it about the guy? He was a freakin' bookie. Why could he look at Anthony and—

Shut the hell up, he ordered himself. *You're here for Rae. Remember that.*

Anthony pulled a chair away from the table to his right, slid it up next to Mr. Pink, and plopped down in it. "Yep. It's me again. I love this place." Anthony waved at one of the waitresses in her short little ref uniform—what all the girls at The Score sports bar had to wear. He reached over, pulled an olive out of Mr. Pink's martini, and crushed it between his teeth.

Mr. Pink looked freakin' amused. "Did you want to place a bet on another nonexistent race?" he asked.

A blush heated up Anthony's cheeks. A friggin' blush. He hoped no one could see it in the dim bar. Most of the light came from the dozens of TVs. "I came here to find Aiden Matthews," Anthony announced.

"I should have tape-recorded our last conversation," Mr. Pink said, sounding bored. "Since I didn't, and you don't look intelligent enough to remember it, I will repeat myself—Aiden Matthews is not here."

"Yeah, I realize that," Anthony answered. "But about twenty minutes after I came in here the last time, Aiden was on my butt. He'd heard I'd been looking for him. How do you think he heard that?"

"Little birdie?" Mr. Pink suggested.

"Little pink birdie," Anthony agreed. "I want to know where he is. And I want to know now."

Anthony didn't see the signal, but there must have been one because a second later he was being pulled out of his chair by a guy that should have been on *WWF Smackdown!* WWF dude marched him out of the bar while all the jerks in the place were hooting and clapping. "Which car is yours?" WWF asked when they hit the parking lot.

"The Hyundai," Anthony mumbled. Because what was the point in drawing the process out?

"Okay, so get in your Hyundai like a good boy, and I'll watch you drive away," the guy said. "And if I ever see you in the same room with my boss again, I'm kicking your butt across the state line."

Anthony followed his orders and got in his car. He started to slam the door shut, but WWF blocked it. "You ever been to The Elbow Room?" he asked.

"The Elbow Room," Anthony repeated. He'd been preparing a little defense action in his head. He hadn't expected a question.

"You should. It's your kind of place." After that, he shut the door for Anthony and gave him a wave. Anthony stared at him for a second, still trying to process, then he backed out of the parking space and hauled butt out of the parking lot. The first gas station he saw, he pulled in and got directions to the Elbow Room.

Can't believe Mr. Pink's guy did me a favor, Anthony thought as he drove to Little Five Points, where the bar was supposed to be. *Unless he didn't really do me a favor. Unless I'm going to be met with a bunch of goons with baseball bats.*

But when he found the crappy-looking little bar, the parking lot only had a few cars. And no goons. *Maybe WWF just found out he has a tumor or something,* Anthony thought. *Maybe he wants to get in a few good deeds in case he kicks it. Whatever. I owe the guy one if I ever see him again.*

Anthony climbed out of the car and strode into the Elbow Room. It wasn't nearly as classy as The Score. No cute little waitresses. And it smelled like someone had puked in the corner not too long ago.

But it's not like he was there for the friggin' atmosphere. He blinked a few times, letting his eyes get used to the dark of the bar, then he scanned the place, squinting at each of the dim figures hunched at the bar.

No Aiden. Crap. He checked the tables. Most of them were empty. There was a guy macking on a woman at the one all the way in the back. And a guy making a pyramid of shot glasses at the table closest to the door. But that was it. No Aiden.

Time to make friends with yet another bartender, Anthony thought. He pulled out a twenty and started over. Then a flash of movement to his left caught his eye. He glanced over and saw Aiden stepping out of the men's room.

Thank you, mysterious bodyguard, Anthony thought as he rushed over to Aiden. "I've got nothing to say to you," Aiden told him.

"Then just listen," Anthony said. He'd been working on a list of all the ways Aiden owed Rae, starting with the fact that Rae's mom was dead because of the agency Aiden had been a part of. But as he stood in front of Aiden, the list slithered out of his mind. "I can't lose her, all right?" he burst out. "She's—Rae's—crap. She's everything. What she's done—what she—"

Anthony sucked in a breath. He sounded like a

freakin' idiot. "If you don't help me track down Yana, Rae could die. And that—" He pulled in another breath, trying to find the words.

Aiden didn't bother waiting. He turned and walked out of the bar.

Chapter 4

"Rae, stop, okay?" Mandy said.

"We're almost there," Rae answered, without looking at her. She was still way too new to driving to look anywhere but the road.

"Stop, okay? Please *stop*!" Mandy's voice rose into a hysterical shriek.

Rae risked a glance and felt her stomach flood with acid. Mandy's face was drained of blood. She looked like she was going to pass out any second.

"Blinker," Rae muttered. "Blinker, blinker." She flipped the turn signal on and checked over her shoulder. "Do you see my blinker?" she shouted at the car behind her. Somebody honked, but Rae ignored him. She slowed down and glared at the guy in the next lane until he let her over. Then she parked next to—okay, half on—the curb. "What's wrong? What happened?" she demanded, taking Mandy by the shoulders.

Mandy didn't answer, but Rae noticed her fingers tighten their grip on the silk blouse she held. Her nails had started to shred the delicate fabric. "Is it your sister?" Rae asked.

"There's something wrong with my eyes," Mandy managed to get out. "I think—Rae, I'm going blind."

"What?" Rae cried.

"All of a sudden it's like I can only see in two circles—like two spotlights. Everything else just went dark." Mandy's voice was shaking so badly, Rae could hardly understand her.

"All of a sudden?" Rae repeated. "You've never, ever experienced anything like this before?" Her own voice was shaking a little, too, even though Rae was trying hard to stay calm.

"Never," Mandy answered. "I was, you know, *looking* at my sister, and when I *came back,* there was all this blackness."

"Do you have an eye doctor?" Rae asked. "I can take you right now. Or to the emergency room." Mandy's face grew even more pale, if that was possible. "If something happens to me, my dad will lose it. After my mom. And if Emma goes off with Zeke.

He'll lose it," Mandy said in a rush, ignoring Rae's question. She rubbed her eyes viciously with the heels of her hands.

"Stop it, okay? Stop it. That's not going to help," Rae ordered. She grabbed Mandy by the wrists and forced her hands away from her eyes.

"It's like everything's dark and there are two flashlight beams and I can only see what's in the light," Mandy said, her hands shaking under Rae's fingers. "What does that mean? What's going on?"

"And it's never happened before?" Rae asked. She knew she was repeating herself, that Mandy'd already answered the question. But it was too bizarre for something like this to happen just bam! Wasn't it?

"No. Never," Mandy answered, her voice rising. She was clearly on the edge. "I told you that."

"Did you hit your head today or . . ." Rae couldn't even think of another possible explanation. What Mandy was describing was so strange. She eased her grip on Mandy's fingers, slowly letting go and resting her hands back in her lap.

"No," Mandy said. "You've been with me most of the day. I've just been sitting around in my room." She glanced down at the blouse, and it was like something clicked in Rae's brain.

"How many times have you used your power to

see your sister today?" Rae asked. "I mean, just in the car you've done it like five times, right?"

Mandy frowned. "I guess. Every time I let go of the shirt, then touch it again, I'm there, I'm here. Sometimes I didn't even decide to do it. So maybe more than five. I kept checking to make sure that she was still at Virgin, even though checking every thirty seconds is stupid."

"That's got to be it," Rae murmured.

"What? What's it?" Mandy asked, the irritation in her tone dissolving back into pure fear.

"I have this side effect when I do my fingertip-to-fingertip thing," Rae explained.

"Right. You said you get numb spots," Mandy said.

"Yeah. And maybe that's what's going on with your eyes. 'Cause the two little circles of vision—that's weird. So weird that it makes weird sense if it's a side effect of using your power. If it is, and it's like mine, it should wear off pretty fast—in less than a day."

"Do you really think that could be it?" Mandy asked.

"It kind of makes sense, don't you think?" Rae said. "Maybe you should give it a few hours to find out if you start to see a little better before you go to the doctor. You don't want anybody thinking you're having some kind of psychosomatic deal. Believe me, the mental hospital is not a place you want to spend time." She released Mandy's wrists. "So how about if I take you home? We can hang there for a while, see if I'm right."

"We're almost at Virgin. I really want you to see what you can find out about Zeke. If my eye thing is what you think it is, it doesn't matter what I do, right?" Mandy shook out her hands, then smoothed her long hair away from her face.

"As long as you don't use your power," Rae agreed.

Mandy handed over her sister's blouse, quickly dropping it on Rae's lap before she had time to connect to her sister. "I can see well enough not to walk into walls. Let's go, okay?"

Rae placed the blouse on the backseat of her dad's car. "Okay," she answered. "But if it starts to get worse or if you start to feel dizzy or anything—"

"I'll tell you, and we'll go straight home," Mandy promised.

Should I be driving her straight to a doctor? Rae wondered as she put on the turn signal to reenter the traffic flow. *What if I'm wrong about what's going on with her? What if a vessel in her head is about to burst or something?*

Rae flashed on the image of Mandy in Rae's

old room at the hospital. It could happen. Mandy could end up there if she started babbling about temporary blindness, especially if she freaked and spewed about her power. *We're talking a few hours to see if she gets better,* Rae reminded herself. She checked the traffic in the closest lane. When it was clear, she inched her way back out onto the street.

"Sorry to park so far away," she told Mandy when she'd driven the three blocks to the Virgin Megastore and maneuvered the car into a space at the back of the lot. "I'm not such a great driver yet. I like to have empty spaces on both sides."

"Doesn't matter." Mandy climbed out of the car. Rae got out as fast as she could and hurried over to her.

"How does it feel to be standing up? You okay?" Rae asked.

"Fine," Mandy answered. "And the circles, I think they're getting bigger. I can see a little more."

"Great, great," Rae exclaimed. "You going to be all right crossing the parking lot?"

"Let me use you as a guide dog just in case." Mandy grabbed Rae's arm with both hands.

"And we're off," Rae said as she started across the lot, going slowly so she didn't steer Mandy into any parked cars. Finally they made it to the massive front doors, and Rae ushered Mandy inside. Immediately Mandy started turning her head back and forth, searching for her sister. "Let me help," Rae offered. "What does Emma look like?"

"Kind of like me," Mandy answered. "Same color hair, but hers is really short, with bangs. Brown eyes, like mine. A little taller. Bigger on top." Mandy gestured toward her chest. "And Zeke—longer hair than Emma's but brown, too. I don't even know what color his eyes are since he spends most of his time glued to Emma's face. And he—"

"I think I see them." Rae took Mandy by the shoulders and turned her slightly to the left. "On the next level up. Is that them?"

Mandy tilted her head back and forth. Rae figured she was trying to get her spots of vision lined up right. Then she nodded, her mouth tightening. "That's them. Let's go."

Rae guided her over to the escalator. When they got to the top, she steered them over to Emma and Zeke.

"Hey," Mandy said, her voice really loud. "What are you guys doing here? I wasn't expecting to see you two."

Not exactly subtle, Rae thought, slapping a smile

on her face. "Hi, I'm Rae. A friend of Mandy's."

Emma gave her a look, like, Why are you friends with a fourteen-year-old? Zeke's eyes, which appeared slightly glazed over, traveled lazily up and down her body.

Might as well do this now, Rae thought. She reached out and shook Emma's hand, feeling like a dork because who shook hands? Then she grabbed Zeke's hand and let her grip slide low enough to bring her fingertips into contact with his.

And she was in a bubble. A liquid-filled bubble. She could see out through its lime-green walls, and everything out there looked . . . pretty. Pretty. And lime green. And sort of bendy. Look! There was a bendy lime-green squirrel over there. Look how its tail stretched out, out, out, bending, swaying, like it didn't have even a thin little tailbone in it.

The squirrel turned its head toward her. Its eyes were bendy, too. They bulged out, out, out. Until they looked like they were going to pop. If they popped, Rae's bubble would pop. She knew it. *Knew it.* And the squirrel knew it, too. The squirrel wanted it to happen. Because the squirrel knew that if her bubble popped, Rae would die. And the squirrel, the pretty squirrel, it wanted her to die.

Its eyes swelled out even farther, like two water balloons getting filled from a hose, fuller and fuller and squishier and squishier. They were going to pop. They were going to pop!

Pop!

Rae blinked, and the world was filled with color again. Mandy had her hand on Rae's arm. *She must have pulled my fingers off Zeke's,* Rae thought. From the squinty-eyed look Emma was giving her and the smirk Zeke had on his face, Rae figured she'd held his hand a little too long. Maybe a lot too long. Thank God Mandy'd broken her grip. If that squirrel had—*The squirrel wasn't real,* she reminded herself.

"I need to go to the bathroom. Come on, Rae," Mandy said.

"We're heading out. So I'll see you at home," Emma told her sister.

"Oh. Oh, well, Rae and I were thinking of going to get pizza at that place you like across the street. You want to—"

"We already ate," Emma said, her voice cold. *Probably because she thinks I was flirting with her possibly soon-to-be husband,* Rae thought. "See you at home," Emma repeated.

"Okay," Mandy said. She let Rae lead her to the bathroom. The second they were inside, Rae leaned over the nearest sink and splashed cold water on her face. She wanted to wash the memory of that evil, freaky squirrel out of her mind. Not that the water would make it from her face to her brain, but somehow it helped, anyway.

Rae straightened up and grabbed a paper towel. As she dried off, she realized there was a numb spot forming over her left eyebrow. *I wonder if I can get spots inside, like on my liver or my kidneys or—*

"So?" Mandy said, practically hopping up and down with impatience.

"So, so I didn't get that much," Rae admitted. She wasn't going to lie to Mandy, even though she sort of wanted to. "I'm pretty sure that Zeke was on a pretty strong drug cocktail. All I got was a bunch of psychedelic garbage. Sorry."

"It's okay," Mandy answered, her voice limp and her whole expression deflating.

Rae's chest squeezed. This girl she barely knew had done so much for her—Rae had to find a way to make sure she didn't let her down.

"Turn left here. Then pull into the dentist's office parking lot," Aiden instructed.

Anthony followed the directions in silence. He and Aiden hadn't talked during most of the trip. Aiden had basically told him where to turn and nothing more. But Anthony didn't care. All that mattered was that Aiden was in the car, period. He still could hardly believe Aiden had walked out of the Elbow Room, gone straight to Anthony's Hyundai, and gotten in.

"This is it. This is where I kept her," Aiden said. He got out of the car. Anthony scrambled out and followed him to the office door.

"Dentist office. Good cover. No one would wonder why there was screaming," Anthony joked. Aiden didn't crack a smile or even give a forced "ha." He just unlocked the door and led the way inside.

"You're going to be disappointed," Aiden said as he locked the door behind Anthony. "There's nothing to see here."

"You didn't think you'd left any clues when you cleaned out your apartment and bolted, remember? But all it took was one push of the redial button to start tracking you down at The Score," Anthony answered.

"Yana didn't have a phone in her room," Aiden told him. "And she was drugged up the whole time I had her here."

"Not too drugged up to escape," Anthony shot back. Aiden didn't have an answer for that. He just waved Anthony down a sterile corridor with pale green walls.

"This is it." Aiden stopped in front of a large

glass window, the kind of glass that was reinforced with embedded crisscrossing wires.

Anthony peered inside. It was empty except for a single bed with a plain blue spread and a freestanding toilet and sink. "Can I go in?"

Aiden nodded, and Anthony stepped into the room. The first thing he did was rip off the bedspread and shake it out. He pulled the pillow out of the case and turned the case inside out. He felt the pillows, hoping to find a little tear that might mean something was hidden inside. But it was smooth and soft under his fingers.

"Next," he muttered as he flipped the mattress. Nothing underneath. He stretched out on his stomach and checked under the bed. Clean. While he was down there, he did a survey of the whole floor. Bare linoleum. No bumps. No pencil marks or anything. Crap.

Anthony stood up and checked out the ceiling. No tiles that could have been pulled down and then replaced. Aiden was right. There was nothing here. And even if Yana had left a print somewhere that Rae could pick up, they already knew Yana could block her thoughts. There was no point in dragging Rae all the way out here. "So there was a power surge and she just waltzed out the back door. Is that right? Even though she was so drugged up?"

"Yes," Aiden answered. The bastard wasn't helping any more than he had to. Fine. Whatever. Anthony had needed him to find this place, but he didn't need anything else. Right now, anyway.

Anthony opened the back door and stepped outside into an alley that was about a car length wide. There was a Dumpster to one side of the door. Empty. "What's the closest public transportation to here?" Anthony asked. "Bus? Train?"

"The bus station's about half a mile away," Aiden answered from inside. "East on Hillary to Curtner. On that corner."

"I'm going there. You coming or staying?" Anthony leaned through the doorway and looked at Aiden.

"Staying," Aiden answered.

"So am I going to have to make friends with every bookie in town so I'll know where to find you if I need you? Or are you going to cough up an address?"

Aiden didn't answer. Anthony crossed his arms and waited.

"I guess I'll be here for a few days at least," Aiden answered. He smoothed a loose piece of hair back into his ponytail. "Safe as anyplace, I guess."

"When you decide to move, I want to hear from

you," Anthony said. "You owe Rae. You know that."

Aiden nodded, but that didn't mean anything. Anthony locked eyes with him for a moment, trying to figure out if he could trust the guy. Aiden gave him nothing back. But it wasn't like Anthony could do anything. He couldn't handcuff Aiden to him until the Yana situation was dealt with. Although if Anthony could have, he would have.

Without bothering to say good-bye, Anthony started down the alley.

"Wait," Aiden called. Anthony turned back, and Aiden threw a pack of matches at him. "It's the number here. In case."

"Thanks," Anthony said. Aiden ducked back inside. Anthony stared after him for a few seconds, then turned and circled around to the parking lot. He climbed in the Hyundai and drove straight to the bus station. If Yana had been here, somebody had to have noticed her, he thought as he got back out of the car, hurried inside the station, and got on the shortest ticket line. Yana didn't exactly blend, not with her bleached blond hair and that tattoo on her belly.

Come on, come on, come on, he silently urged the guy ahead of him who was carefully counting his change. The guy placed the money in his wallet in what seemed like slow motion, then finally left the window. Anthony stepped up and slapped a photo of Yana that he'd gotten from Rae down on the counter. "You seen that girl around? The blond, not the one with the curly hair?" he asked.

The clerk studied the picture for a second, then nodded. Anthony felt a surge of adrenaline, and he leaned in close to hear what she had to say. "She was sleeping on that bench over there when I got on shift at midnight last night," the woman said, gesturing to a nearby wooden bench. "I almost went over and woke her up. It's not a safe place for any woman to sleep. And someone as young as her? Forget about it."

"So what happened to her?" Anthony asked, unable to keep the urgency from his voice. "Did she just leave or what?" He felt like yelling, but if he did, the woman probably wouldn't be in the mood to help him, so he tried to sound concerned about Yana, in a big brother kind of way.

"Nope. She bought a ticket from me this morning, when I was about to get off."

"To where? Do you remember?" Anthony asked.

"Atlanta. Like half the people I sell tickets to," the woman answered. She popped a stick of Big Red gum in her mouth.

"So she's there already?" Anthony gripped the counter with both hands.

"Yeah," the woman answered, chomping away. "She'd have gotten in hours ago."

Crap. Crap. Yana's there. I'm here. Rae's got no one to protect her.

Rae tiptoed across the front lawn, the dewy grass slick and cool under her feet. Before she'd made it halfway to the sidewalk, Anthony was out of his car. He raced toward her like she was the goalpost on a football field. "What happened?" he demanded, his voice low and intense.

"Nothing. Nothing bad," Rae answered quickly. "It's just that if you're going to keep watch on me all night, you might as well come in. Your back's going to kill you in the morning if you don't. The coach will be really pissed."

Rae didn't care about the coach. But she didn't want to just say, "Hey, Anthony, you want to come in and spend the night in my bedroom?"

"What about your dad?" Anthony asked, squinting.

Rae inched her wet feet onto the tops of his dry sneakers and wrapped her arms around his waist for balance. "He's asleep, and he sleeps like a rock. I'll set the alarm and make sure you're up and out before he gets up. Okay?"

"Okay." Anthony started toward the house. Rae rode on his feet all the way to her bedroom.

"I'll make you a bed on the floor," she volunteered. Although God, how nice would it be to sleep all wrapped up in Anthony's arms. Except that if she *was* all wrapped up in his arms, there was no way she'd ever be able to go to sleep. Rae got a flash of an up-all-night kind of night with Anthony. She wanted that. Someday. Someday when they wouldn't have to worry about Yana hurling herself through the window and trying to kill them both.

Rae grabbed one of her pillows and tossed it onto the floor. "There are some extra blankets in the closet," she told Anthony. "Sorry I don't have a sleeping bag. My dad and I, we're not exactly outdoor types."

Anthony stood rooted to the floor, looking at her, and Rae was pretty sure he was thinking almost the same thing she'd been thinking a few seconds before. The realization made her feel like she'd chugged a pot of steaming tea. Heat flooded her entire body. "Closet. Right." Anthony jerked around and retrieved a couple of blankets from her top shelf.

"Sorry I don't have anything you can sleep in," Rae said. She ran her hands down the oversized T-shirt she wore to bed. "I have lots of these, but they wouldn't exactly fit you. Well, they'd fit you. But they'd be tight. Like the T-shirt you already have on. So it wouldn't—" *Stop the babbling,* she ordered herself. "It wouldn't make sense," she finished.

"I'm . . . what I have on is fine," Anthony told her. He knelt down on the floor, spread out one of the blankets, then slid off his shoes without bothering to untie them and lay down.

"I guess I'll turn off the light," Rae said.

"Yeah," Anthony answered.

Rae slid into bed and switched off the lamp on her nightstand. "So, good night."

"Good night." Rae heard Anthony roll onto his side. Should she pretend to fall asleep right away? Or should she talk, the way she would if Yana was sleeping over? Yana back when Yana was her friend. When Rae *believed* Yana was her friend.

"How did it go with Mandy?" Anthony asked.

"Uh, not great," Rae admitted. She rolled onto her side, too. If they'd both been on the floor or both been on the bed, they would have been face-to-face. "Actually, she got me pretty freaked out on the car ride. She's having this blind-spot thing, I guess sort of like my numb spots. But it got a little better over a couple of hours, so I think she'll be okay, probably by tomorrow. She just has to be careful not to use her power a lot."

"Huh." Anthony paused, and Rae figured he just didn't know what to say. As great as Anthony was, having an ability that changed your life like that was pretty much something you had to experience to totally get. "Did you find anything out at least?" he asked. "About Zeke?"

"No. When I went fingertip-to-fingertip with him, I couldn't get much because he'd ingested or inhaled or smoked or whatevered enough to block pretty much everything. The top layer, what I could get to, was just bizarre images." Rae decided not to describe the squirrel. It wasn't something she wanted to think about right before going to sleep.

"You ever, you know, do any of that?" Anthony asked.

"No, never," Rae replied. "I think the whole thing with my mom, thinking she was a killer, it made me want to stay under control. I was always afraid I had that—that killer part in me and it could come leaping out, like some kind of deranged jack-in-the-box, if I wasn't careful. You know, I've never even gotten drunk, if you can believe that."

"You're not missing all that much," Anthony answered. She heard him roll over again so that he was facing away from her. "At my old school I was smoking weed every day. I only stopped because I finally decided I wanted to graduate sometime before retirement age."

"Are you waiting for my gasp of horror?" Rae

teased. Because the way Anthony had said it, it was like a huge confession.

"The college professor's daughter and the pothead. It doesn't exactly sound like friggin' Romeo and Juliet. I mean, Mandy's all upset because Zeke's using," Anthony answered.

"First, a lot of college professors' daughters *are* potheads," Rae answered. "Probably a few professors, too," she added with a smile, thinking of some of the ones she'd met through her dad. "And second, Mandy's freaked because her sister's stopped caring about stuff she used to care about. She's thinking about dropping out of school, even. And from what Mandy said, getting a scholarship's something Emma's been focused on for years."

Rae leaned over the bed and ran her palm down Anthony's back. "If you're thinking that you're bad for me or some bull like that, stop it," she said softly. "You're the perfect guy for me. You're the opposite of Zeke."

Anthony snorted.

"I mean it." Rae ran her hand up his back. "Like the swimming thing. I was afraid to even step into the shallow end when I met you. And now I can kick and breathe and everything."

"It's not a big deal," Anthony said.

“Yes, it is,” Rae insisted. And it was. Anthony was everything she could ever want in a boyfriend—even though he was nothing like the perfect guys she used to imagine. She just hadn’t known what perfect was back then.

Chapter 5

Every muscle in Anthony's body went tight. He cracked his eyes open just a slit. There was somebody in the room. Not Rae. He could hear her soft breathing on the bed behind him. Someone else. Over by the window.

He opened his eyes a fraction farther. Without lifting his head, all he could see was a pair of feet in camouflage-print sneakers. Did Yana have shoes like that? Anthony couldn't remember. His brain felt as tight as the muscles in his body. It was hard for thoughts to squeeze through. But it had to be Yana, right? Mandy wouldn't be stupid enough to come sneaking in now that she knew Yana was on the loose.

Okay, so I've got to take her down before she

gets in my brain. Gotta be something fast. Something that will knock her out—ba boom. Nothing came to him. Not one friggin' thought.

The feet in the camouflage sneakers began to move toward him. *All right, so, so I let her get closer,* he decided. *Then I do a snatch and jerk on her closest foot. She hits the floor. Probably won't knock her out. But she'll be surprised. That might give me a couple of seconds. No time to look for a weapon. Just gotta grab her head and slam it against the floor. Only gonna get one chance. If she's not out after one hit, I'll be her puppet boy for the rest of my life.*

"Which won't be very long," a voice said. Yana's voice. Not possible. Or could she read minds, too?

"There's nothing I can't do," Yana answered, even though he hadn't spoken aloud. "You should have stuck with me, Anthony. You could have had anything you wanted. Except your little rich-girl arm-trophy."

Anthony tried to sit up, but his body wouldn't respond. She had him. She already had him.

"Yes, I do," Yana said. He watched her feet move toward him. That's all he could do. Watch. Wait for whatever it was she had planned. "On your back," she ordered.

Instantly Anthony was on his back. Yana knelt beside him. She lowered her face to his. And then she was kissing him. And he was kissing her back. He didn't want to. But his lips, his tongue, they weren't under his control.

"Oh my God," Anthony heard Rae cry out. "Oh my God, what are you doing?"

He couldn't answer. All he could do was keep kissing Yana. Bile splashed up his throat and into his mouth. He hoped Yana could taste it, that it would disgust her. But she cupped his face in his hands and kept on kissing him. Deeper. Harder.

"This is sick. This is just sick. Get out of my sight, both of you," Rae yelled.

Didn't she understand? How could she think that he'd be doing this willingly? What did she think he was?

Yana pulled her lips away from Anthony's and smiled down at him, her breath hot against her face. "She thinks you're a loser, Anthony, that's what she thinks," Yana whispered. "And she's right. You can't even protect her from me."

Yana leaned in closer so that her lips were brushing against his with each word. "I own you." She ran her finger through his hair. Then he felt her nails scratching against his scalp. Digging. "I own you," Yana repeated. And her fingers plunged through his scalp, broke through the bone of his skull, and clawed into the flesh of his brain.

Anthony let out a shriek of agony. Yana grabbed him by the shoulders and shook him. "What's wrong? Anthony, what's wrong?"

Wait. That wasn't Yana's voice. It was Rae's.

Anthony opened his eyes and saw Rae staring down at him. "That must have been one bad nightmare," she said, brushing his sweaty hair off his forehead.

"Yeah," Anthony answered.

"Want to tell me about it?" Rae asked.

"No," Anthony blurted. "No. I'm okay. You should go back to sleep."

Rae returned to her bed. Anthony rolled onto his side and faced the window. There was no way he was going back to sleep tonight. He wasn't taking his eyes off that window. He wasn't even going to friggin' blink. Because Yana was wrong—or the Yana in his dream was wrong. Anthony *could* protect Rae. Could and would. Or he'd die trying.

"Mandy and I were all over Atlanta Underground. And nothing," Jesse Beven said. He ate the last of his Chick Filet curly fries and started in on Anthony's, as usual. If the kid wasn't kind of his honorary brother, Anthony would've had to deck him.

"A bunch of the people who worked in the stores knew Yana or had at least seen her around. But not in the last few days," Mandy added. "You two have any luck?" she asked Rae.

"We got nada," Rae said. She picked up a fry, started to take a bite, then let it fall back onto her plate. Her face was pale, and there were dark smudges under her eyes. This was getting to her. Big time.

"Hey, finding out where she isn't isn't nada," Anthony answered. Rae, Mandy, and Jesse all looked at him like he was a friggin' idiot. Which he was. A friggin' cheerleader idiot. There was no point in pretending they weren't in deep crap here. That wasn't going to help Rae.

"So, what next?" Mandy asked. She grabbed a napkin and leaned toward Jesse, going for the streak of ketchup on his chin. Then she froze and reached for her Dr. Pepper, like that's what she'd been going for all along. A blush was working its way up her neck. Anthony glanced at Jesse. He was blushing, too.

Rae gave him a kick under the table, and when he looked at her, she smiled in a way that told him she'd noticed the little Jesse-and-Mandy minidrama, too. Man, Anthony'd never heard Jesse even mention a girl before—except for that actress who played Meadow Soprano. Jesse was obsessed with her. But an actual girl he'd actually met . . . Jesse definitely hadn't ever gone there before.

"Um, what're we doing now?" Mandy asked again.

"Yana goes to the stores in Little Five Points a lot," Rae answered. "And I guess we could check out the Happy Burger, where she works. There are probably a few places around there that she hangs out."

"Anthony and I will take the Burger," Jesse volunteered.

Mandy's mouth opened, like she wanted to say something, but she just took another sip of her soda. *Why doesn't he want to team up with her again?* Anthony wondered.

"So Mandy and I will go to Little Five Points. You want to meet back here in a couple of hours?" Rae asked. She met Anthony's gaze, and it was like she knew exactly what he was thinking, knew exactly how freaked out he was about the idea of her being anywhere without him. "Remember, nobody's going to approach Yana," she said. "If any of us see her, we get everybody together and make a plan before we do *anything*."

Anthony leaned into Rae. "You sure you don't want me to come with you? Mandy and Jesse—"

"I think it will be fine," Rae cut in, giving him another look that seemed to say there was a good reason for Jesse to go with Anthony instead of Mandy and she knew what it was. "I'll be okay. You can't be with me every second."

Jesse licked his finger and poked around on his

plate, gathering up all the microscopic fry bits. "Ready to roll?" he asked Anthony. He licked the fry bits off his finger. Classic Jesse.

"Yeah." Anthony stood up. "See you back here," he told Rae. Like by saying it, it would absolutely be true. Like the words would actually make it absolutely impossible for anything bad to happen to her that would stop her from meeting him. Like freakin' magic. "See you back here," he repeated. He couldn't stop himself. Then, before he could say it five or ten or a hundred more times, he strode out of Chick Filet, Jesse right behind him.

They got in the car, and Anthony headed for the Happy Burger. He didn't think Yana would be there. Who would hang around work if they didn't have to? But maybe she had a friend at the place who would have some ideas about where Yana might be. And Anthony'd rather be doing things that didn't have much of a chance of working than doing nothing.

"Um," Jesse said. That was it. Just *um.*

"What?" Anthony asked.

Jesse started drumming on the dashboard. "You going to go see that Jim Carrey flick?"

"I'm not going to spend any time sitting in a dark place staring in one direction while a homicidal psycho is on the loose," Anthony told him. He hadn't meant to sound so pissed off. But what was Jesse thinking?

"Yeah. Right," Jesse said. He stopped drumming and flicked on the radio. A couple of songs went by, then Jesse started up again. "Um."

"Spit it out," Anthony told him.

"Do you think Mandy would like that movie, the Jim Carrey one?" Jesse asked, staring out the window like he'd never seen a sidewalk or trees or people before. Like they were freakin' fascinating.

"Looks funny," Anthony answered. "But gross. You really want to be sitting next to a girl watching something that's ninety percent fart jokes?"

"I didn't say I wanted to go with her," Jesse protested, turning back toward Anthony. "I was just asking if you thought she'd like it."

Anthony narrowed his eyes at him. "Okay," Jesse said. "Okay, I was thinking about asking her to go with me." He turned back toward the window. "So what do you think?"

Anthony paused. A few weeks ago his first response would probably have been that Mandy was way out of Jesse's league. He'd seen where Mandy lived. A girl like that usually didn't go out with a guy who'd been forced to go to group therapy because he kept setting things on fire. But girls like Rae didn't usually go for guys like Anthony, either. And besides—Mandy seemed pretty cool, not like someone who would care about all that stupid crap.

"Bad idea?" Jesse asked when Anthony didn't say anything.

"No, you should go for it," Anthony answered. "I mean, maybe choose more of a chick-friendly movie. But you should do it." Anthony grinned. "I think she liiikes you," he teased as he pulled into the left lane. The Happy Burger was coming up.

"Look!" Jesse cried. He grabbed Anthony's arm so hard that Anthony almost lost control of the wheel. "Yellow VW coming out of the Happy Burger lot. Could be Yana's."

"I'm on it." Anthony shot a glance at the oncoming traffic, then pulled a U and started after the Bug. He tried to get a glimpse of the driver, but he was blocked.

"She's changing lanes. She's gonna turn," Jesse said.

Anthony switched into the right lane, ignoring the honks coming from behind him. He was sure that if it was Yana up there, she'd seen him by now. But he didn't care. Yeah, they'd agreed not to approach Yana without a plan, but he couldn't let her get away.

The yellow Bug made a right onto a residential street. No other cars were in sight. Good. Anthony put on the gas. The yellow Bug sped up, too. "You're not getting away from me," he muttered. He floored it. He pulled up alongside the Bug. If he had to, he'd jerk his car in front of hers. He didn't care if the Bug hit them—as long as it stopped Yana.

"It's not her!" Jesse shouted. "It's some guy."

Anthony let up on the gas. He pulled over to the curb and stopped. His nerves felt like he'd spent the afternoon getting fried in an electric chair. "Where the hell is she?" he burst out. And worse—what did she have planned for Rae?

It felt bizarre being back in Atlanta. It was like it was a place she'd lived in a long time ago. Like one of the dozen of crap holes her dad had dragged her to. Not like the place she lived now. Not like home.

Yana started walking faster. *Once you do what you've got to do, you can live wherever you want. You can leave Atlanta behind.*

Yeah, right. As if she'd have a choice about whether or not to leave town after she'd gotten her revenge. She'd have to leave because there would be a whole platoon of people hunting her down, wanting to shoot her down like she was some kind of rabid dog.

I might never make it out of Atlanta alive, she thought. But it wasn't like she cared that much. If they killed her—fine, whatever. As long as she got to do her killing first.

Yana broke into a trot. She was so close. She just wanted to get there and do it. *Get there. Do it. Get there. Do it.* The thoughts repeated over and over in her mind to the rhythm of her footfalls. She turned the corner. This was it. This was the block. She was so, so close.

"For you, Mom," Yana whispered as she started across the Wilton Center parking lot.

A guy fell in step beside her, probably around sixteen, Asian, spiky black hair. "I'd say, judging by the musculature and general attitude, kickboxing," he said.

"Do I know you?" Yana asked. Why was he talking to her? God, all she wanted was to get inside. Get there. Do it.

"No, but you should. I'm Sam," he answered. "So was I right? Are you here for kickboxing class?"

Yana stopped walking. "No," she told him.

"Hmmm. Have you gone the other way, perhaps? Decided to deal with your aggression with a meditation class?" Sam asked.

"The reason I stopped walking wasn't so you'd keep trying to hit on me. It was so you'd go away. Just so you know," Yana said. She crossed her arms and waited. She couldn't do what she had to do with this freak trotting after her.

Sam laughed. She noticed that the skin underneath

his chin was loose and jiggly, even though he wasn't at all overweight. Skinny, actually. "I'm not hitting on you," he protested. "Your pheromones just don't call out to mine—no offense. I'm sure lots of guys go for your type."

Bull. Yana knew when a guy was checking her out, and Sam was checking her out.

"You ever heard that expression, 'When the student is ready, the teacher appears'?" Sam went on. Like she actually cared what he had to say. He didn't wait for her to respond. "Well, I think you're ready, so—" He stretched out his arms in a here-I-am gesture.

Enough. She'd been waiting most of her life for this moment. She wasn't going to let freakboy slow her down. Get there. Do it. Get there. Do it. It was as if her heart was speaking those words as it beat.

TAKE A WALK AROUND THE BLOCK. NOW. She hurled the thought at Sam. And he turned on his heel and left her. Finally.

Yana locked her eyes on the front doors of the Wilton Center and didn't look away until she'd reached them. In this place, down in their little rat hole in the basement, were the government bastards who had killed her mother. Yana pushed her way through the doors and headed straight to the stairs. She knew right where to go, thanks to that visit she'd made here with Rae.

Rae. God. Even thinking about her was like drinking acid. *I could have killed her. I could have killed her, when she's just like me.* Yana shoved the thought away. Now wasn't the time. If she made it out of here alive, then she could apologize to Rae. Yana snorted. Yeah, right. An apology would make everything all better. Maybe she should go all out and cough up two bucks for a Hallmark card. Because that would definitely make the fact that Yana tried to make Anthony feed Rae rat poison forgivable.

Yana reached the door leading to the stairs. She twisted the knob. The door was locked. Not a problem. Yana walked directly to the closest classroom. She stuck her head in, ignoring the senior citizens making collages. "I need you to unlock the door to the basement stairs," she said. She repeated the words in a thought bullet to the teacher's head. *I NEED YOU TO UNLOCK THE DOOR TO THE BASEMENT STAIRS.*

"I don't have the key," the teacher answered.

"Who does?" Yana asked. *TELL ME.*

"The security guy. In the room at the end of the hall. The door on the left," the teacher said, massaging her temples with her fingers.

"Thanks." Yana marched down to the security station. The beefy guard didn't look happy to see her. Guess he didn't want to miss any of the *Sex and the City* rerun he had on one of the TVs he was supposed to be monitoring. *Unlock the door to the basement stairs.* Beefy guard stood up with a grunt and obediently headed toward the stairs. "Good boy," Yana muttered as she followed him.

Come on, come on, come on, she thought as he reached the door and started fumbling with the mess of keys on his key ring. She wanted to get down there. Get it done. Get down there. Get it done. If she had to wait even a few minutes longer, she was afraid a vein would burst in her head or something. Every part of her body and mind was focused on getting the revenge her mother deserved. Yana had been waiting so long.

The guard managed to unlock the door. "You can go now," Yana said. "I've seen the episode you were watching. If you don't hurry, you're going to miss a great Samantha scene." *Go.* The good boy left. And Yana started down the stairs, knees trembling. God, she was close.

She reached the landing, turned—and froze. Waiting for her at the bottom of the stairs were three men and a woman in riot gear. They each had a semiautomatic trained on Yana. "Put the guns down," she ordered, her voice cracking.

They didn't move. They all kept the guns on

Yana. *I only said it,* she realized. *I didn't think it.*

PUT THE GUN DOWN. PUT THE GUN DOWN. PUT THE GUN DOWN. PUT THE GUN DOWN. She blasted each of the four of them as hard as she could.

And the guns stayed aimed at her. None of the guards even twitched. *PUT THE GUN DOWN. PUT THE GUN DOWN. PUT THE GUN DOWN. PUT THE GUN DOWN.* Yana shot the thoughts at them, using every bit of energy she had. Blood started to trickle out of her nose.

But the guns stayed up.

And the guards started toward her.

Chapter 6

UNLOCK THE DOOR.

Neither of the government goons even glanced at the doorknob. Big surprise. Yana'd been shooting out thoughts all over the place, and nothing. Her head felt like it had imploded. *Now what am I going to do? What in the hell am I going to do?*

Also, what in the hell were *they* going to do? Two of the men, still in their riot gear, had stashed her in a large office. Now they were just standing on either side of the door. Both watching her. Not saying anything.

Yana leaned back in the armchair. Then she used her feet to pull the ottoman in front of the chair beside hers over in front of her. Her heart was beating out a drum solo, and a muscle in her thigh had started to twitch. But she wasn't going to let these guys—anyone—know how scared she was. That would give them power over her.

Maybe I should slip off my sneaks, too, Yana thought. But that was probably going too—

The sound of the door opening jerked her away from her thoughts. Yana forced herself to hold her ultrarelaxed, screw-you pose as a fiftyish man walked behind the desk in front of her and sat down. One side of his mouth curved up as he looked over at her. Suddenly Yana felt like a stupid little kid trying to act tough in front of the principal.

"I'd like you to tell me what you're doing here," the man said. "I'm Mr. Eggar, by the way."

You lie. You tell the truth. Those were her only two options. She was trapped. "I'm Yana Savari," she answered. "My mother was Erika Keaton." She'd decided to start with truth. She didn't think there was any way that Eggar and the boys were going to believe she'd come to the center for a knitting class and gotten lost. "Do you know who Erika Keaton was?" she asked.

You should, you bastards. You killed her, Yana want to scream. But she didn't.

"Yes," Eggar answered. "But Erika Keaton had no children. So why don't you try again?"

"You did a pathetic job on the tracking," Yana shot back. Eggar's eyes widened a fraction. "Yeah, I know you were tracking all the offspring of the women in your group. G-2s, that's what you call us, isn't it?" She was feeling less like a little kid every second. *Don't get too cocky,* she reminded herself. *You surprised him, yeah. But there are two guys with guns over there.*

Eggar gave a little flip of his hand, signaling her to go on. He was doing a decent job of pretending that she hadn't just rocked his world.

"My mom left town when she was pregnant," Yana continued. "After I was born, she handed me off to a friend." *Like some stupid letter she wanted mailed,* Yana thought. She cringed inside. It hadn't been her mother's fault—Erika had only been trying to protect her. "Long story short. The friend died, and I got reunited with dear old dad. Who didn't even know he had a kid. We moved around a lot and ended up back in Atlanta, where the beautiful love story of Erika Keaton and David Savari had begun."

And I started trying to figure out how to get revenge, she thought. Her mother had left a letter for her, a letter Yana had gotten ahold of years before she was meant to see it. She'd learned everything—about the group her mom had been in, about how Erika worried her life was in danger and that's why she needed Yana to have this letter just in case. Yana'd even read about the power she could possibly develop when she was older, the power she *had* developed. Once she'd read the letter, she devoured everything she could find about Erika Keaton. Unfortunately, she ended up being fed just what "they" would have wanted her to see if they'd known she was out there—all the clippings about Erika's murder by Melissa Voight.

Yana kicked the ottoman away and sat up straight. Her brain had gone there so many times since what almost happened with Rae in the cabin, and she couldn't do it anymore.

"When I was about twelve, I started getting my power," she said. "I was an early bloomer." Time to switch to lie. She hoped all the truth she'd blurted would make them swallow the next part. "I've figured out a lot of what I can do. But I bet there's more. I want to learn. And you're the only ones who can teach me. That's why I'm here."

If he buys it, I'm safe—for now, Yana thought. *If he doesn't, I could end up with a bullet in my brain.* She locked eyes with Eggar. What was it going to be?

Rae stabbed a spinach leaf with her fork. It was humongous. There was no way she'd get it past her lips without a bunch of unattractive lip gymnastics. But she couldn't pull it off the fork and choose a smaller piece. That'd be so tacky. And Mandy and her family seemed to take dinner seriously. They had candles and place mats—stuff Rae and her dad never bothered with. She glanced around the table from Mandy to Emma to Mr. Reese. None of them was looking at her. She risked it, jamming the leaf far into her mouth and then using her tongue to wrangle it all the way in. She gave a few hard chews, then tuned back in to the conversation.

"Have you been either place, Rae?" Mr. Reese asked.

"Um," Rae mumbled, trying to finish chewing.

"Italy or Alaska," Mandy said, helping her out. "We're trying to figure out which one we should go to over summer vacation."

"You two are trying to figure it out," Emma said. "I'm not going."

"It's a family vacation, Emma," Mr. Reese told her.

"I know that," Emma answered. "But I'm eighteen. I'm past the age where I want to spend the summer with dad and little sis."

Great. She's in a pissy mood already, and Mandy and I haven't even gotten a chance to get her alone and talk to her about Zeke, Rae thought. She really hadn't thought that sitting Emma down for a chitchat was a good idea, anyway. But Mandy wanted to give it a shot so badly, and she was convinced having Rae there could help somehow. So how could Rae say no?

"I've been to England," Rae said, leaping into the conversation. "My dad loves England. He teaches medieval literature at the university. His big thing is Arthurian legends, so England is like heaven for him." *You can stop now,* Rae told herself.

"Your father's a professor?" Mr. Reese asked.

"Uh-huh," Rae told him, not letting herself start to spew again.

Mr. Reese looked over at Emma. "Maybe you could talk to him, Em. He might have some suggestions about summer reading that would help you get a jump at UCLA."

"Sure," Rae volunteered. "He lives for that kind of stuff."

"I'm full," Emma announced. She left the table without another word.

"I apologize fo—" Mr. Reese began.

"Don't apologize for me," Emma muttered as she went through the dining-room door. She shut the door behind her before he had time to respond.

"You know what, I'm pretty full, too," Mandy said. "Or at least full to the point that I think it's time for me and Rae to retire to my room with a pint of New York Super Fudge Chunk." She stood up. "Is that okay?" she asked, starting to sit down again.

"Fine," her father answered, staring down at his plate as though there was a secret message hidden there.

"Okay, then. Come on, Rae. To the kitchen," Mandy said, her voice full of false cheeriness.

"To the kitchen," Rae repeated. She followed Mandy.

"New York Super Fudge Chunk is Emma's fave," Mandy said when they reached the fridge. "I figure it will at least get us into her room." Mandy pulled a pint of ice cream from the freezer, then opened a drawer and grabbed three spoons. "Here we go."

Mandy took the lead again. She barged into Emma's room without knocking. Not the way Rae would have gone. "I brought ice cream," Mandy announced. She plopped down on Emma's perfectly made bed, then tossed a spoon at her sister.

Emma caught it, hesitated a moment, then sat down next to Mandy. "Don't pick out all the white chocolate," she warned.

"I'm eating *some* of it," Mandy answered. She patted the bed next to her, and Rae headed over and sat down. "I met this guy," Mandy blurted.

No segue. No finesse. Mandy and Rae had made

a plan to work the conversation around to guys, yeah. But talk about obvious. *She's nervous,* Rae reminded herself. *She's completely freaked out about the Emma-and-Zeke situation.*

"*You* met a guy?" Emma asked. She pried a chunk of white chocolate out of the rock-hard ice cream.

"Yeah. *I* met a guy. He's really cute. And he's the same age as me. And he rides a skateboard," Mandy said in a rush.

She's talking about Jesse, Rae thought. She would have known that even if Mandy hadn't mentioned the skateboarding part. She'd seen the way Mandy was looking at Jesse at the Chick Filet. Rae'd felt that same expression on her own face when she looked at Anthony.

"And you know what the best thing is about him?" Mandy hurtled on. "He makes me feel like I can do anything. Is that how you feel about Anthony, Rae?"

It really sounds like she memorized a script. Rae shot a look at Emma. Emma didn't seem to have realized she was being set up. At least not yet.

"Yeah. Anthony's always totally behind me," Rae answered. "Whatever I want to do, he wants to help. Like swimming—" *Or like helping me figure out what my power was,* Rae added silently. "He's teaching me to swim because I love taking long baths, but I was afraid to step into even the shallow end of a pool."

Again, too much information. But it didn't come out sounding rehearsed, at least. It came out too dorky to be rehearsed.

"Is that how it is with Zeke?" Mandy asked.

Here we go, Rae thought.

But Emma seemed eager to talk about Zeke. "When I'm with him, I don't know, it's like there's a heat lamp switched on inside me. And when I'm not, the lamp's off and everything is grayer and colder."

Mandy shot Rae a glance that was easy to read, a look that shouted out, Oh my God. Mandy'd clearly come to the same conclusion Rae had—Emma was completely gone, completely gaga, completely in love with Zeke.

Mandy jammed her spoon into the ice cream so hard that it knocked the carton out of Emma's hand. "Sorry," she muttered. She leaned over, grabbed the carton, then returned it to Emma. Rae thought she saw Mandy's fingers trembling.

"It . . . it sounds great with Zeke," Mandy said. "But is it like Rae and Anthony? If there was something you wanted to do, would it be important to him? As important as it is to you? Because that's how it seems like it is with Rae and Anthony. And I think, I hope, that's how it might be with me and this guy someday."

"Yeah. Definitely," Emma answered.

Mandy shot Rae another panicked glance. Rae knew Mandy wanted her to say something. But what? Emma was never going to see anything bad about Zeke. That was obvious.

"Really?" Mandy went on when Rae didn't jump in. "So like when you head off to UCLA, would he, I don't know, would he rent a U-Haul and drive your stuff? Would he move to LA to be with you? Would he quiz you on your homework for UCLA?"

Too much. Way too much, Rae thought. But there was nothing she could do to stop the train wreck.

"You've been listening in on my phone calls again, haven't you?" Emma demanded. She shoved the ice cream carton at Mandy. "Did you tell Dad what you've heard?"

"If I had, you'd be locked in your room permanently," Mandy answered. "But you're insane if you think Zeke really loves you. If he did, he'd want you to take the scholarship and—"

"Get out," Emma ordered, her voice low and cold. "Right now. Both of you."

* * *

The sting of the electric charge hit Yana's temple. "What is it?" Eggar asked, holding up a playing card with its back to her.

Yana had no clue. Her brain felt like a melted blob of ice cream. "What is it?" Eggar repeated.

Slowly Yana managed to find the words she wanted. "Two of spades," she answered, taking a wild guess.

Eggar placed the card on the table between them, faceup. Seven of hearts. "The electric stimulation doesn't seem to have any effect. Let's move on."

Move on? God, weren't they finished? If they kept going, her brain wouldn't just be a blob. It would be a puddle. Yana yanked off the electrode that had been taped to the side of her head. Out of the corner of her eye she caught a flash of movement. She turned toward the window that looked out onto the hall, expecting to see some other agency suit. But it was Sam. The freakboy who'd glommed on to her in the parking lot yesterday. He was wearing a T-shirt with a chimp on it. Someone had drawn a table around the chimp and added restraints to its hands and feet. The guy pointed at Yana, pointed at himself, then pointed at the chimp, like they were three of a kind. Then he turned and walked away.

"Who was that?" Yana asked.

Eggar got up and shut the blinds. "You don't need any distractions," he told her.

"I need a break. That's what I need," Yana said.

"If you are serious about discovering the depth and range of your powers, you—"

Eggar was interrupted by the door swinging open. A woman in a suit that screamed money, money, money stepped inside. Instantly Eggar stood, gathered his notes, and left. The woman sat down across the table from Yana and smiled. "Is Eggar treating you all right?" she asked.

"He's okay," Yana said.

"Good, good," the woman answered. "Did you sleep well last night? Is there anything I can get you? Change of clothes? Some food you've got a craving for? I get a serious craving for biscotti right around this time of day. The ones that have been dipped in chocolate."

Oh, so you're going to be the good government agent. You act all concerned about me, and then I'll do whatever you want, right? Yana thought. *Well, I'm not that easy.*

"Who are you?" Yana asked.

"Silly me." The woman smoothed her deep red hair away from her face with her perfectly manicured nails. "I'm Layla Cascone. I'm the administrator of this facility. We're all very glad you found your way to us. I know we can help you reach your maximum potential."

And then what will you have me do with it? Yana wondered. That was the million-dollar question. She didn't ask it, though. She just nodded.

"I have a quick question for you, then I think you can call it a day. You look wiped out," Cascone said. "I was wondering how you were able to find us."

Yana definitely wasn't going to tell Cascone that Rae had brought her here. In fact, she'd do whatever it took to protect Rae from these government goons.

Yeah, and she'll really appreciate that, Yana thought. *She'll appreciate how loyal you were to her and forget all about how you tried to, what was it? Oh, right—kill her.*

"My power—" Yana began.

"Wouldn't give you that kind of information," Cascone finished for her. "I really must have a satisfactory answer." She picked up the electrode that had been taped to Yana's head and twiddled it between her fingers. "And I'd much rather have you tell it to me than have to go digging for it." She set the electrode down in front of Yana.

Threat received, Yana thought. Cascone could be bluffing. There might be no possible way to shock the info out of her brain. And she'd learned over time that she even had the ability to block her thoughts from others. Rae had never been able to read a single fingerprint of hers. But why risk it? Yana had an answer she thought would work.

"A guy named Aiden Matthews told me where to come," Yana answered.

Anthony headed into the gym. He didn't want to be going to football practice. He wanted to be out hunting Yana down. But if he skipped practice, he'd get the coach angry. And if the coach got too angry, Anthony'd be shipped out of Sanderson Prep and back to Fillmore High. Which meant he wouldn't be at school with Rae, and he wouldn't have the tiniest shot in the world of not turning out a supreme loser. That couldn't happen.

He hitched his backpack higher up on his shoulder and headed down the row of lockers. "I can't believe you screwed me over," a voice said from behind him. Before Anthony could turn around, somebody gave him a vicious shove. He stumbled backward, hit the bench behind him, and went down. Before he could shove himself back up, Marcus Salkow was on top of him, one of his knees pressing on Anthony's chest.

"You knew how I felt about Rae, and the second we split up, you're all over her," Marcus yelled.

"Get off him, Salkow," McHugh ordered Marcus. He hauled Marcus up, and Anthony scrambled to his feet. "The coach is going to show any second."

"You know what this liar did to me?" Marcus demanded, glaring at Anthony.

"You ask me, he did you a favor," McHugh answered. "Rae's psycho. She could snap at any second. If you'd stayed with her, you could've ended up without a head."

"*You* could end up without a head if you're not careful," Marcus told McHugh.

Sanders joined the group, already in his sweats. "Ease off, Marcus. You know you didn't want her anymore. You said yourself that you—"

"Shut up, Sanders," Marcus cut him off.

Anthony took a step closer to Marcus. "You didn't deserve her."

"And you do?" Marcus asked. "You're a lowlife. You can barely read. You wear clothes from Kmart. And you've decided you're better than me?" He moved in on Anthony, getting so close that they bumped chests.

"She chose me, didn't she?" Anthony asked. It was all he could say. Everything Marcus had spewed out was true. He locked eyes with Marcus and didn't blink until Marcus looked away. Then Anthony turned and walked over to his locker, going plenty slow enough to show Marcus that he wasn't running away.

Anthony heard the guys calming Marcus down. Telling him Rae wasn't worth it. Anthony wasn't worth it. He tried not to listen, changing into his workout clothes as fast as he could. He wanted to be out on the field. He could only pray that Marcus was on the other side during the scrimmage. It would feel so good to take that smug jerk down.

He slammed his locker shut, clicked the lock in place, then headed to the double doors leading to the gym where they always warmed up. The guys were silent as he passed them. *Guess I won't be going partying with the team anymore,* he thought. Not that he'd want to after today.

Anthony reached for the door handle, and his eyes went to the pay phone next to the door. He decided to give Aiden a quick call. He didn't have a cell phone, so Aiden wouldn't be able to call him until tonight. That was too long to wait for an update.

Quickly he dropped some change into the phone and dialed Aiden's number. He'd memorized it as soon as he'd gotten it. "It's me," he said as soon as Aiden picked up.

"You got my message. Good." Anthony didn't interrupt to say he hadn't gotten any message. "I know where Yana is. She's with the—"

Anthony heard the sound of plastic hitting wood. The phone went flying, he realized. Then he heard a muffled scream, so high and long, it made all the hair on his arms stand straight up.

"Aiden, what happened?" he shouted, praying the guy could hear him. "Are you okay? What happened?"

The only answer was silence.

Chapter 7

Rae set her cell down on the dashboard after about the fiftieth time she'd tried Aiden since Anthony'd picked her up. "No answer," she told Anthony.

"We're almost there," Anthony said. His voice was calm, but he had a death grip on the steering wheel. "See that dentist's office up on the left? That's it."

There was no ambulance parked outside. No groups of rubberneckers. Nothing out of the ordinary on the street. Rae wasn't sure if that was a good sign or a bad one. *Aiden's okay,* she told herself. *He's been trained to take care of himself. Maybe he just . . . fell and knocked himself out, and that's why he isn't answering the phone.*

Anthony pulled into the dentist's office parking lot and parked in the spot right in front of the door. Rae was out of the car before he had a chance to get the key out of the ignition. She raced to the entrance and twisted the doorknob. Locked. Rae twisted the knob harder, using all her strength, ignoring the burst of static that pushed through her head—noise with no clear thoughts. Nothing that could help her. She had to get inside. Now, now, now!

"Aiden, are you in there?" Anthony yelled. He stepped up behind Rae and pounded on the door. "Aiden, come on! Answer us!"

Rae and Anthony both listened hard. But there was no answer from inside. No sound of movement. "Let's try the back." Anthony sprinted around the building, Rae right behind him. Her heart cramped as she saw the back door hanging from one hinge. Somebody'd broken in.

Anthony jerked to a stop. He held up one hand, signaling Rae not to go any farther. "We don't know if whoever did this is still in there," he whispered.

"If they are, they must have heard us pounding on the front door," Rae whispered back. "But we have to risk it. We have to get in there."

Anthony nodded, then he crept toward the open door. Rae twisted her hands in the back of his T-shirt and followed. Just inside the doorway, Anthony paused. Rae listened hard. But she didn't hear anything except her own harsh breaths.

Anthony took another step. Then another. Rae's breaths came faster each time they moved forward. *Get a grip,* she ordered herself. *You hyperventilate, you faint. And you're not going to be able to help Aiden if you're sprawled out on the floor.* She focused on pulling in a long, slow breath and then calmly letting it out. In. And out. In.

Rae's fingers tightened on Anthony's shirt. "Do you smell that?" she asked, her nose automatically wrinkling in disgust at the putrid stench.

"It's urine," Anthony replied, no emotion in his voice. He took another step into the hallway.

Yeah, that was it. The smell of urine. But there was another smell mixed in. Metallic. Thick. It brought up a taste in the back of her mouth—warm and salty.

Blood. That was the other smell—blood. "Aiden!" Rae screamed, not able to hold the cry back.

There was no answer.

Rae let go of Anthony and bolted down the hall. "Aiiiden!" she screeched again, so loud, she felt the soft tissue inside her throat begin to fray.

"It's—he's in here," Anthony called. Rae spun around and saw Anthony standing in the doorway of a room she'd run right past. The expression on his face made her body feel like it was filled with slush—cold, gray, dirty. It was only about ten steps back to Anthony, but it felt like there were miles and miles between them. *Get back there,* Rae ordered herself. *Get back there, now! Aiden needs you.*

Except, if there was anything to do for Aiden, Anthony wouldn't be standing there looking at me, a little voice inside Rae muttered. Rae ignored it. She concentrated on crossing the distance between her and Anthony. Between her and the room where Aiden was.

"Don't." Anthony grabbed her arm when she reached the doorway. "You don't need to see it. Him."

"He needs help," Rae insisted. She pulled free from him and rushed into the room before he could stop her. Aiden . . . Aiden lay on the ground, still, so still, his head turned away from her. Rae dropped to her knees next to him. CPR. That's what he needed. CPR. Why was Anthony just standing there? Didn't he have a clue?

Rae took Aiden's head in her hands and turned his head until he was looking up at the ceiling. Now what? Now what?

The answer came to her almost immediately. She'd practiced this over and over on a big plastic doll when she took first aid last year. Tap the shoulder. Call his name.

Rae slammed her fist down on Aiden's shoulder. "Aiden!" she shouted. "Can you hear me?"

No response. Now what?

"Stop it, Rae," Anthony said. But he sounded far away. Rae didn't bother to answer him. He didn't understand what she was doing. He didn't know how important it was.

Now what? she asked herself again. Tilt the head. That was it. Rae pulled up on Aiden's chin and pressed down on his forehead until his head was in the correct position for CPR. It was hard. His neck was hard to flex. But she did it. Next. What next?

"Rae, come on." Rae felt Anthony's hands on her shoulders. She didn't look up at him. She was trying to think. *What next?*

Clear the airway. That meant open the mouth. Anthony started to pull on her shoulders. "He needs CPR," she snapped. She used both hands to pry Aiden's mouth open.

There was something in there. Something blocking the air. No wonder he wasn't breathing.

Rae gingerly reached into Aiden's mouth and latched onto the object. She gave a tug and pulled it free. It was . . . paper. A ball of paper.

"Can I see that?" Anthony asked.

Rae didn't answer. She had to continue the CPR. Every second was crucial. *Do I start pressing on the chest or do mouth-to-mouth?* She couldn't believe she couldn't remember. What was the point of learning this if you couldn't remember it in an emergency?

Just do something, she told herself. She lowered her mouth to Aiden's. Before their lips could meet, Anthony hauled her to her feet and turned her to face him. "Aiden's dead, Rae," he told her. "He's dead. There's nothing you can do. Nothing anybody can do."

Rae twisted around and looked at Aiden's body. His *corpse.* How could she have thought for one second he was alive? He was already getting stiff. She should have realized that as soon as she touched him. And the blood, there was so much blood. It was on her hands now, on the legs of her khakis.

"You okay?" Anthony asked.

"Yeah," Rae answered, still staring at Aiden's body. "Yeah," she repeated, forcing herself to turn her gaze back to Anthony. "I guess I . . . I just wanted him to be alive." She had to push the words out through a salty lump of unshed tears.

"I know." Anthony reached for her hand. "Can I see that paper?"

Rae involuntarily tightened her fist. "Let me do it," she answered. She willed her fingers to loosen, then uncrumpled the ball of paper. It was a note. A note to her.

Black dots exploded in front of Rae's eyes. She blinked rapidly until they disappeared, then read the words on the damp, wrinkled paper.

Rae, forget about us. Or die.

Anthony sat on Rae's bed, waiting for her to get out of the shower. She'd been in there awhile. With the amount of blood she'd gotten on her, it made sense. Yeah, it must all be washed off by now. But he bet she could still feel it.

He got a memory flash of her, crouched over Aiden's body, her hands on his face, his dead eyes staring up at her. He should have tried harder to keep her out of that room. She didn't need to have a vision of Aiden's corpse locked in her head for the rest of her life.

"Penny for your thoughts." Anthony jerked his head toward the bathroom door. Rae stood there, her hair still damp from the shower, feet bare, a strained smile on her face. "I guess I'd be wasting my money, though. I already know what you're thinking about. Aiden."

Anthony nodded. Rae walked over to the bed and sat down next to him. She took his hand, and he noticed she was careful not to let her fingertips touch his. She hadn't put the wax back on them yet. "It doesn't matter," he told her, looking down at their clasped hands. "You know everything about me, anyway."

"Still, privacy," Rae answered. She let out a sigh. "So."

"So," Anthony said back.

"I guess we should talk about it." Rae's grip on Anthony's hand tightened.

"Yeah," he agreed. The whole ride back, they'd listened to the radio in silence or made stupid little comments about nothing to each other. But they couldn't keep pretending nothing had happened.

"Got to be the agency people who killed him," Rae said.

"Yeah. They must have found out that he was hiding Yana." The smell of blood and urine filled Anthony's nose again as he thought about Aiden. The smell of death.

"And that he was trying to help me," Rae added. "Clearly they knew that I was in contact with him." Her eyes strayed to her desk. The note was hidden inside.

It's like I helped kill the guy, Anthony thought. *I begged him to help Rae, and now he's worm food.* "Don't start thinking it's your fault or anything," he told Rae, talking to himself as much as to her. "The guy helped us, yeah. But it's not like he was clean. He was there when they were doing the experiments on your mom. He knew Mercer was killing people. And he didn't try to stop it."

"He stopped the agency from killing me. Or whatever they were going to do when they busted into that motel room where I was meeting Mercer and killed him," Rae reminded Anthony. "They would have at least locked me away for the rest of my life."

"Yeah." What else could he say? He wanted to say something brilliant, something that would somehow make everything okay, but there was nothing.

Anthony let go of Rae's hand so he could wrap his arms around her. He pulled her close enough that he could feel her heart beating against his chest. The clean grapefruit perfume she always wore filled his lungs as he breathed in, and it washed away some of the death smell.

He could deal with the fact that Aiden was dead. It wasn't like he was happy about it or anything, but he could deal. Aiden had sort of had it coming.

But if Rae—he cut off the thought before he could complete it and buried his face in her damp hair. She tightened her arms around him.

Freeze time, he thought. He didn't need anything else to happen to him in his life. *So just somebody freeze time now.*

* * *

Go home and act like everything's normal. Easy for her to say, Yana thought. She walked across the lawn toward her house. It looked different to her. Like she'd been away for a million years. But it had only been a couple of weeks.

Wonder if Dad even noticed I was gone, she thought as she unlocked the front door. *Probably,* she decided when she saw what a sty he'd made of the place. He had to have noticed there was no one following him around with a shovel.

So I'm supposed to have a normal life—except for my power-training sessions, Yana thought. She shut the door and stepped into the living room. That's what Ms. Cascone had told her. *I guess that means I should—*

"Yana? Is that you?" Before she could answer, her dad strode into the living room and got in her face. "Where in the hell have you been?"

Like you care, Yana thought. "At a friend's. You're always saying how you want more privacy for you and what's her name, so I thought I'd give you two a little honeymoon."

"If you're not going to be here, I expect a call," he told her, sounding like he was doing an imitation of a dad on a sitcom. Which he probably was. It wasn't like he had a clue on his own.

"Fine. Next time I will. Sorry," Yana said. She could

thought-implant him and end this conversation right now, but it felt like her brain had freezer burn.

"You don't sound very sorry," he went on. But his dad imitation was already getting shaky. He missed his French toast and his meat loaf; she was sure of that. Other than that and the cleaning thing, she could have been locked in her room for weeks for all he knew.

"I am sorry," Yana answered. Even to herself she didn't sound sorry, but she kept on going. "It was inconsiderate." That's what a sitcom dad would want to hear. "I really won't do it again. Now I've gotta go to bed. School in the morning."

Without giving him a chance to reply, she stepped around him and headed straight to her room. It felt different to her, too. Smaller. But God, she was glad to be there. She'd been sure she'd never get out of the Wilton Center alive when she'd realized that everyone in the agency could somehow block her thought-implanting.

Didn't matter. She had permission to go there every day. More than permission. The goons would probably hunt her down if she didn't show. And somehow she was going to figure out a way to take the whole place down. For her mom. And for herself. And even for Rae—not that Rae would ever let Yana within a hundred miles of her again.

Yana shoved off her shoes without untying them, then stripped off her jeans. She fell into bed, wearing the T-shirt she'd had on for way too many days. All she wanted right now was sleep. But her bed didn't feel right. She rolled onto her side so she was facing the wall and rearranged the pillow under her head. It didn't help. She flopped onto her back. The new position didn't feel comfortable, either.

I should be able to sleep on a pile of rocks, Yana thought. *That's how tired I am.* But she felt all itchy. Maybe she should have changed the T-shirt. Yana sat up and flicked on her dim bedside table light.

Movement from the other side of the room caught her eye, and she froze. Had they followed her? She blinked, looking over in the direction of her desk.

"Oh my God," she whispered. The pen on her desk, it was writing all by itself. *You fell asleep,* she told herself. *You don't remember, but you fell asleep, and now you're dreaming.*

The pen stopped writing and dropped off the desk. It bounced when it hit the floor. *You fell asleep,* Yana told herself again. But it didn't feel like she was asleep. Her skin had broken out in goose bumps. That didn't happen in a dream, did it? And things didn't look so sharp and clear and basically *normal* in a dream, did they?

"You know you're not dreaming, so just stop it,"

she said aloud. She forced herself to stand up, then she walked over on trembling legs to the pen. She picked it up. It lay still in her hand, the plastic barrel cool.

Yana set the pen down on her desk and stared at it, waiting for it to move again. It didn't. Maybe she really had been dreaming. What was she thinking? Of course she had been. It was the only explanation. She pulled out her desk chair and sat down. She needed to rest before she took the few steps back to her bed, that's how weak her legs felt.

I'll just put my head down for a few minutes, she thought. Then she saw it. The note. The note the pen had been writing.

Stay away from the Wilton Center if you value your life.

Chapter 8

Yana parked her Bug between two SUVs, then climbed out and slammed the door. "Welcome to the world of boring rich people," she muttered. If she had the money that the people at this school had—Yana shook her head. She shouldn't be thinking about that bull, especially not after what that kind of thinking had almost made her do. She shuddered, reminding herself that she was here for a reason. And just where was her reason? Yana scanned the groups of people leaving Sanderson Prep. No. No. Nope. *Did I get here too late?* She looked from face to face to face.

Ah, there you are. Yana strode across the parking lot. Anthony saw her coming and rushed to meet her. Before she could say a word, he shoved her against the nearest car, another SUV, of course.

"What are you doing here?" he burst out. "I'm telling you right now, you even think about hurting Rae, I will kill you."

Yana tried to pull away, but Anthony's fingers were digging into her shoulders. "Look, I found out the—"

"What kind of twisted bitch are you?" Anthony demanded. "You'd actually kill an innocent person for something you thought her mother did? Are you brain damaged?"

Yana squeezed her eyes shut and tried to let his words wash over her. But he was saying all the things she'd been thinking.

"All Rae wanted was to be your friend," Anthony continued to rant. "That's it. And you—"

"If you don't want to find your hands around your own throat, let me go," Yana said. She opened her eyes and stared at him. He stared back for a moment, his brown eyes hot with anger. Then he released her and took one step away. "You have no right to judge me. Your mom's still alive," she told him.

"And that excuses everything?" he asked. "That makes it okay that you—"

Yana didn't want to hear whatever he was going to say next. "My dad said you were looking for me. That's why I came here," she interrupted. "I want you to stay the hell away from my house and my father. And stay the hell away from me." That was all she had to say to him. She never wanted to see his face again. When he looked at her, she couldn't take what she saw in his gaze. Everything she'd already told herself so many times was right there in his eyes. Yana turned and started away from him. But he grabbed her by the elbow and spun her back to face him.

"I don't care what you make me do to myself," Anthony said, his voice low and harsh. "There's no way I'm leaving you alone unless you kill me. I'm going to be watching you every second. And if you even think about Rae—"

"I'm not going to do anything to Rae," Yana burst out. "If you would just listen, I was trying to tell you that I found out the truth. I know that Rae's mom didn't kill my mom. I'm going to leave her alone. I'm going to leave you all alone. All I want is for you to leave me alone, too."

Anthony didn't answer.

"Well?" Yana snapped.

"Oh, was I supposed to actually believe something you said?" he asked. "Everything that's ever come out of your mouth has been a lie. Everything you've said to Rae. Everything you've said to me. All lies."

"Well, people have been lying to me, too," Yana muttered.

"Not me. Not Rae," Anthony replied, crossing his arms over his chest.

"Right, not you two. You're friggin' saints, okay?" Yana shot back. "I'm not. My mom is dead, and the people who killed her are not going to have a chance to do it to anyone else. But you and Saint Rae can just go on with your lives and be fabulously happy." Yana glanced at some of the prepsters milling around. "Although don't be surprised if she dumps you for one of the white-bread rich boys eventually." Yana turned around again and walked away—fast, so he couldn't grab her again.

"You're going after the agency?" Anthony called after her.

Yana kept walking. She had to get away from here. Away from him. She couldn't spend another second thinking about Anthony or Rae or anything else except finding a way to take the agency down.

"Yana, that's suicide." Yana heard Anthony hurry up behind her. He didn't touch her this time, and she kept walking. "They just killed Aiden Matthews. And they made it clear they'd kill Rae, too, if she didn't keep her mouth shut about them."

Yana took another step. Her foot slipped off her platform sandal, and she stumbled. Before she could catch her balance, she fell, skinning her knee on the asphalt of the parking lot. Tears stung her eyes. She blinked them away. But more kept coming, and a trail of snot started dripping out of her nose.

Stop it, Yana ordered herself. *Now.* She wiped her sleeve across her eyes and nose, hard, and shoved herself to her feet. Then she turned and faced Anthony. "Aiden's dead?"

"Yeah. And Rae got a warning that if she even talks about the agency, she'll end up dead, too," he answered. "They'd have no problem squashing you like a cockroach."

"I can't believe he's dead. I was with him. . . . He was . . ." Yana's words trailed off. She couldn't remember what she'd meant to say. Her brain was all fuzzy all of a sudden. She bit the inside of her cheek until the pain pulled her out of her personal fog. "They killed him because they thought he helped me, right?"

Anthony shrugged, not looking at her. "I doubt they were happy that he quit. Or tried to. I don't think it's really a place you can leave."

Blah, blah, blah. What he was really saying was yes. The inside of her nostrils began to sting, and she knew in another second she'd be bawling again. "I gotta go," she muttered. Her car was just a few feet away. All she wanted to do was get in it and get out of the parking lot before she lost it.

Aiden helped with the experiments, she told herself.

It's not like he didn't deserve it. A scalding tear splashed down onto her cheek. Yana reached her car and yanked open the door.

"Don't be stupid, Savari," Anthony called as she slid into the driver's seat.

"I don't care what happens to me anymore," Yana answered without turning her head. "As long as I can make those bastards pay."

Rae was in the zone. She wasn't thinking anymore, wasn't using any "art math," any the-space-between-Anthony's-eyes-is-a-fraction-less-than-the-width-of-one-of-his-eyes kind of calculation. Nothing like that. Well, probably deep in her brain she was still plotting out the ratios, trying to get the proportions right. But it felt like her hand just knew what to do and all Rae had to do was let it go. And right now her hand was everywhere on the sketch pad, erasing little sections to show the highlights in Anthony's dark hair, shading the curves of his ear, lightly erasing his irises so they were pale enough for the blue of his eyes.

Wait. Rae's hand jerked, and the pencil flew out of her hand.

"I'm that ugly, huh?" Anthony teased, taking the opportunity to break out of his pose and stretch.

"No, of course not," Rae muttered as she felt

around her desk chair for the pencil. Anthony grabbed her hand. "Hey, what's wrong?"

"Nothing," Rae answered. She tried to pull her hand away so she could keep feeling around for the pencil, but Anthony wouldn't let go.

"That's bull. I can see your face. What's wrong?" Anthony asked again.

Rae turned her sketch pad toward him. "Notice anything?"

"It's good," Anthony answered. "You're really good. Not that I know anything about it."

"The eyes. Look at the eyes," Rae urged. Couldn't he see it?

"I guess they're a little lighter than mine . . ." Anthony began. "Am I supposed to be seeing something else? I told you, I don't know anything about—"

"They're Yana's eyes," Rae interrupted. "I drew Yana's eyes in your face." She turned the sketch pad toward her and stared at the familiar eyes. Looking at them made the back of her neck prickle.

"So erase them," Anthony said.

"Yeah, okay," Rae answered. She grabbed a big eraser off her desk but couldn't touch the paper with it. Her hand started to shake.

"What?" Anthony sounded impatient. "What, Rae?" he asked again, more gently.

"They look so scared," Rae told him. "Yana's

eyes look so scared." She couldn't stay away. She knew it then. She'd promised Anthony she would, even after what he told her about Yana's intention. But she was already in this too deep, and there was just no way she could keep her distance.

"Can I come in?" Rae asked.

"No," Yana told her, trying to hide her shock. The last thing she'd expected when she swung open her front door was . . . this. And the last thing she'd wanted, too. She could feel her friggin' eyes stinging already. Wasn't there some kind of limit on how much you could cry in a day? 'Cause there should be.

Rae raised her eyebrows. "Um . . . okay. So what if—what if I just stand here and talk to you for a sec?" There was fear in her eyes and in her voice. Rae was still afraid of her.

Yana nodded in reply, as if someone else was making her head move for her. She wanted to say no again—just looking at Rae got her way too close to losing it—but how could she? Yana should be doing anything Rae wanted. Anything. And she wasn't even letting her in the house. So if Rae needed to stand here and blast her the way Anthony had, tell her what a despicable person she was, then Yana would listen.

"I'll keep it fast," Rae said. "Anthony told me that you're going after the agency. Don't do it."

Yana blinked. "Why do you even care?" she blurted.

"Good question." Rae looked at Yana steadily for a moment, like she was trying to come up with an answer. Trying and having a hard time. "Because . . ." Rae let out a long sigh. "Because . . . You know what? I don't even know. I shouldn't care. You tried to kill me. Thanks for saying you're sorry, by the way."

"There wasn't—what exactly was I supposed to say?" Yana demanded. "There should be, I don't know, different words. Sorry's what you say when you step on someone's foot." And yes, ladies and gentlemen, Yana was crying again.

"So you could have gotten me a Hallmark card," Rae said, the anger drained out of her voice.

Yana snorted, trying to regain control before she started to bawl. She couldn't believe this. Rae was actually being nice to her. Was the girl even human?

"Going back to your other question, I care because a lot of the same things happened to you and me. But I had it easier. I had my dad. Who knows what . . ." Rae's words trailed off.

"Who knows what you would have turned out like if you'd had a dad like mine?" Yana asked. "That's what you were going to say, wasn't it?"

Rae shrugged helplessly. "I guess so," she admitted. "Anyway, it doesn't matter why I care. I'm here, and you should listen to me. You're only one person. You can't go up against the agency and win."

"I can't just do nothing," Yana said. She wiped off her face with the neck of her T-shirt.

"What's going on in your head? Do you even have a plan?" Rae asked.

Over Rae's shoulder Yana noticed an unfamiliar car slowing down as it approached her house. Her heart turned to rock as it pulled into her driveway.

"What?" Rae asked.

Yana's heart slowly returned to beating flesh as the car used the driveway to start a U-turn. *But that could have been anybody,* Yana thought. *God, the agency people could have me under 24/7 surveillance for all I know. If they see Rae with me—*

"You have to leave. You talked. I listened. Now go," Yana snapped.

"That's it? Just go?" Rae asked, her blue eyes widening in astonishment.

"You said what you had to say, didn't you?" Yana asked. She had to get Rae out of there. If the agency spotted them together, then later, after Yana did what she had to do, they might think Rae was involved. And then they'd kill her.

"I said it, but I don't think you got it at all. Whatever your plan is—if you even have one—isn't going to be good enough," Rae said, her voice getting louder and louder. "Those people are professionals, Yan. They—"

Yana gently shut the door. She watched through the peephole until Rae finally turned around, headed down the front walk, and disappeared from sight.

I wonder if I'll ever see her again, Yana thought. But at least one thing was certain—once Yana was through, Rae would never be in danger again.

Chapter 9

Aiden's dead, Yana's sneakers seemed to whisper as she walked down the main hallway of the Wilton Center. *Aiden's dead. Aiden's dead. Aiden's dead.* Knowing that, knowing that the agency had killed one of their own, made the center feel more threatening. Not that she hadn't always known the place was dangerous for her. But now it was more real somehow. Everything felt different. The paintings on the wall done by the art students seemed drained of color. The sound of the guitar class practicing sounded mournful.

They could have played at Aiden's funeral, she thought. *Because Aiden's dead. Aiden's dead. He got what he deserved,* she reminded himself. She wasn't going to waste any tears over him. Yeah, after she'd almost offed Rae, the guy had taken her in instead of handing her over to the cops or to the agency. *But it's not as if—*

Yana jerked to a stop. Had Aiden done more than that? Had he *sent* her that note? She didn't know exactly when he died. God, maybe that was the last thing he'd done. Maybe—

You've got no reason to think that, Yana told herself. *If Aiden had the power to move things around with his mind, he would have used that to bring you down when you had Rae trapped in the cabin.*

So who got that note to her? Someone from inside the center? Who else could it be? How many people on the outside even knew the place existed? The back of Yana's neck started to itch. Was whoever it was watching her right now? Did they already know she'd ignored the warning? What were they going to—

Shut up, Yana thought. *So someone doesn't want you here. Someone with powers. Who gives a crap? You have powers, too—not that you can use them in here. And you're going to show up here every day until you figure out how to shut the place down.*

"For you, Mom," Yana whispered. She started walking again, her shoes immediately starting their Aiden's-dead thing again. She ignored them. Yeah, the guy was dead. But that didn't change anything. She had to do what she had to do.

She turned the corner and immediately saw a guard stationed at the door to the stairs that led down to the basement. *He's waiting for me,* she realized. *Isn't that sweet?* When she reached him, the guard opened the door and gestured her inside. "The guard in the upstairs observation center is now blocked," he told her as she started down the stairs ahead of him. "He won't be able to follow your *orders* anymore. So don't bother trying it."

"Don't be checking out my butt back there," Yana replied, not giving him the satisfaction of commenting on the upstairs-guard sitch. She picked up the pace, taking the steps two at a time. She got to the basement door half a flight of stairs before the guard and started to go inside, but the door was locked. The guard took his sweet time getting over to her. *Yeah, you're big and important,* Yana thought. *You don't have to talk to me. And you can make me wait, gee, a whole minute before you let me in. I'm just so in awe of your power.*

The guard finished punching in the security code, blocking his hand with his body so Yana couldn't see, and swung open the door. Ms. Cascone was waiting on the other side.

Did she put in the order to kill Aiden? Yana wondered. *Did she do it herself?* Yana could picture Cascone's hands with their perfectly manicured nails closing around Aiden's throat. *Although probably she wouldn't have gotten that close. Probably she'd have used a gun.* How had Aiden died, anyway? Anthony hadn't said, and it didn't exactly seem like the time for Yana to push him to "open up" about anything.

"Are you ready to start work?" Cascone asked. Something in her tone made Yana think it was the second time she'd asked the question.

"Yeah. Definitely. So what are we going to do today? Are you going to teach me to get a volcano going with my mind?" It was a completely dorky question. But Yana couldn't stop her tongue from flapping away. Hearing herself talk made the place less creepy somehow.

"Nothing so dramatic," Cascone answered. She started down the hall, not bothering to look and see if Yana was following her or not.

"Oh, so maybe I'll melt a dish of ice cream with my mind," Yana said.

Cascone didn't bother to answer that one. Not that Yana blamed her. She opened the door to a room similar to the one she'd been in the last time, except that this one had a large one-way mirror covering most of one wall. Through the glass Yana could see a large German shepherd trotting around a room with a slew of dog toys scattered across the floor.

"We'll go back to exploring what other abilities you may have in a few days," Cascone told her. "Right now I want to work with you on your mind control. Have you ever attempted to control an animal?"

Yana raised an eyebrow. "Do I look that kinky?"

Cascone didn't even crack a smile. She sat down in one of the metal folding chairs and placed her clipboard on her lap. "See if you can get the dog to pick up the ball," she instructed. "Have a seat if you'll be more comfortable."

"I'm fine." Yana looked through the glass at the dog. His tail was up and wagging. And he, unlike Cascone, was smiling. *Don't be an idiot,* Yana told herself. *He's a dog. His mouth is just shaped that way.*

"Concentrate, Yana," Cascone said, tapping her clipboard with the edge of her pen.

Yana strode forward until she was about half an inch away from the glass. *GET THE BALL.* She aimed the thought right between the dog's pricked ears. The dog cocked his head, like he'd heard something. Yana tried again. *GET THE BALL.*

The shepherd whined. It trotted back and forth across the room. But it didn't pick up anything.

"I think it's receiving something from you." Cascone made a note on her pad. "Try modifying the way you make the command. I'm assuming that you usually use words, am I right?"

"Yeah. Like I thought, 'Get the ball,'" Yana answered. She didn't see any reason to lie. For now she wanted to look cooperative and eager to learn from the great Layla Cascone.

"Mmm-hmm." Cascone made another note. "When working with an animal, it's more useful to send the command in images. So instead of thinking the words 'get the ball' and sending them out, try picturing a ball as sharply and with as much detail as you can."

Yana studied the ball lying to the left of the dog. Then she closed her eyes and tried to re-create the ball in her mind. A tennis ball. Green. With a layer of peach fuzz. *Okay, good,* she thought. She added the dog to her mental picture, the dog with the ball held in his sharp white teeth, the green tennis ball now with a trail of drool on one side. *Got it.* She pushed the image out of her head, aiming it through the glass of the one-way mirror.

The dog gave a sharp bark, and Yana opened her eyes. The shepherd was running in a circle now. But he wasn't stopping at any of the toys.

"I think we should get you a little help," Cascone said. She walked over to the intercom by the door and hit the talk button. "We're ready for Dr. Kessler in eleven C."

A doctor? What was up with that? Yana definitely

was not happy about a doctor being summoned, but she wasn't going to let Cascone know that. Cascone seemed like the kind of person who could find a way to use any scrap of info against you. Yana plopped down in one of the metal folding chairs, trying to look like she hadn't even heard the call for a doctor.

She didn't have to hold her casual pose for too long. A few minutes later the door swung open and a woman carrying a leather bag and a square metal box walked in. She had her long hair in a ponytail, and if Yana hadn't already known the woman was a doctor, she wouldn't have guessed it. Ponytail looked more like a gym teacher, all bouncy and athletic looking. She handed the metal box to Cascone, then pulled up a chair next to Yana and sat. "You've got to be Yana. I'm Dr. Susan Kessler," she said. "Call me Susan, okay?"

"Okay," Yana answered. But most of her attention was on Cascone, who was punching a code into the keypad on the metal box. What could be in there that needed a freakin' *code*?

"I'm just going to get your blood pressure," Kessler said as she pulled a cuff out of her leather bag. She wrapped it around Yana's upper arm and pumped it up until it bit into Yana's skin. Then Kessler let the pressure out slowly, her fingers on Yana's wrist to get a pulse.

"Nice and slow. You deal well with stress, don't you?" Kessler commented as she removed the cuff and stuck it back in her bag. Yana didn't answer. She was trying to see what Cascone had pulled from the box. She couldn't. Cascone was blocking whatever it was with her body.

"Now we'll just get your temperature," Kessler said as she placed a high-tech thermometer in Yana's ear. When the thermometer beeped, Kessler removed it and made a note, then she used a small flashlight to check Yana's pupils.

"I think we're ready to begin," Cascone announced. She strode over to Kessler. Yana's stomach tightened when she saw a syringe in Cascone's hand.

"There are still some more tests I need—" Kessler began.

"You'll have time for that later," Cascone interrupted. Kessler bit her lip, but she rooted around in her bag and pulled out a length of rubber tubing. She knotted it around Yana's upper arm, then swabbed the inside of her elbow with alcohol.

"This is an exciting moment for all of us," Cascone said. "Yana, this drug has been years in development—we only have a few samples available. And you'll be the first to use it."

Yana flashed on the chimp T-shirt Sam had been wearing the last time she saw him. "The first?" she asked. "Wasn't there a lucky monkey somewhere? Or at least a rat?"

Cascone laughed. "Of course it's been thoroughly tested." She handed Kessler the syringe.

Yana didn't want whatever was in that syringe in her body. But there was nothing she could do. Cascone might use the word *us* and act like she and Yana were partners. But they both knew that was bull. As long as she was in the basement, Cascone and her little helpers could do exactly what they wanted.

"Make a fist, please," Kessler instructed.

Yana obeyed. She kept her eyes on her arm and watched as the needle slid into one of her veins, not allowing herself to look away, not allowing herself to even blink. *That's right. Show no fear,* she told herself. Kessler pushed the plunger of the syringe down, shooting God knew what into Yana.

A line of heat moved up Yana's arm. It raced across her shoulder, up her neck, and across the side of her face and then plunged deep into her brain. A moment later she felt her head begin to . . . to *ripple.* It was like something was crawling around between the bones of her skull and the skin of her scalp. Yana reached up her hand, but Cascone grabbed her by the wrist before Yana could feel if the top of her head was actually moving.

"I know the sensation is strange," Cascone said.

Like hell you do, Yana thought. *Like you'd ever let anybody pump this crap into you.*

"But try to ride it out. We only have a short window of time available to us," Cascone continued. She lowered Yana's arm to her side and gave her hand a little pat. "It's better already, isn't it?"

The movement under her scalp slowed down. Like whatever was crawling around up there had gotten tired. "What I want you to do is to try to get the dog to pick up the ball again. Use an image, the way you did before," Cascone instructed.

Yana closed her eyes. She saw the ball. She saw the dog. She saw the drool on the ball. The image was sharper than before. Each droplet of drool glistened like a diamond. She could see each individual hair on the tennis ball. Her eyebrows scrunched together as she hurled the picture out of her head.

"Very nice," Cascone said softly.

Yana opened her eyes. They went straight to the dog. He had the ball in his mouth, and his tail was wagging so hard, it was almost a blur. *I'm like friggin' Doctor Dolittle,* Yana thought. But the communication only went one way. She had no idea what was going on in the dog's head. Except that he looked happy.

Cascone made a note in Yana's chart. "Now, let's try

something a little more difficult. I want you to get the dog to make a circle out of its toys. Don't do an image for each toy, just picture the end result you want."

Yana studied the toys lying on the floor around the dog. Plastic hedgehog, rawhide bone, stuffed cat, the ball, a rubber mailman, a braided rope. She closed her eyes, re-creating the toys in her mind. In her imagination she could see the teeth marks on the bone, the broken whisker on the cat. God, she could almost see the molecules of rubber in the mailman. Whatever had been in that cocktail had done something. Was it permanent? What—*Think about it later, when you're out of this place,* Yana told herself. She flung the image toward the dog. Was it her imagination, or had it actually made a sucking sound as it left her head?

"Very, very nice," Cascone murmured.

Yana opened her eyes. The hedgehog and the bone were already in the positions she'd pictured. The dog quickly added the rope, cat, mailman, and ball to the circle. Then he sat down, looking very pleased with himself.

"We won't be needing you any more today," Cascone told Dr. Kessler.

"I really think—" Kessler began.

Cascone cut her off with a look. Kessler picked up her bag, gave Yana a smile, and rushed out of the room. Cascone walked over to the one-way glass and pulled a gray curtain across it, blocking the dog from view. "Good work, Yana," she said as she headed toward the intercom. "We're almost through. I'd just like us to try one more thing."

Us. Yeah, right, Yana thought.

"This is Ms. Cascone. Please send Sam to me," Cascone said into the intercom.

The door opened instantly. Sam had to have been waiting right outside. What was his deal? Was he one of them? One of the kids of the group?

"Sam, Yana. Yana, Sam." Cascone waved Sam toward the seat next to Yana. He gave her a mocking half bow, then sat down.

His skin looked even worse than it had the other day. It was a pasty color, and there were these patches of sagging skin on his face and his arms and probably everywhere she couldn't see. Last time only the flesh under his chin had been loose. Yana forced herself to look away. The guy was wigging her out. And he was staring at her now—she could feel it.

Cascone walked over to Sam's other side and started whispering to him. At least it got Sam's eyes off Yana. But she didn't like the whispering thing. Were they talking about her? What was the deal? Were they planning something? Were they planning to kill her? She pulled in a deep breath, trying to will herself back into at least the shallow end of the crazy pool. *That's right. Breathe. Breathe.* Yana pulled in a breath so deep, it made her lungs ache.

God, what's that smell? she thought. The answer instantly popped into her head. That smell was Sam. Or at least it was coming off Sam. It was like—it was kind of like that mouse she'd found under the fridge that time, the one that had been dead for at least a couple of days. The same sweet, rotten, decay smell was coming off Sam. Yana felt bile rise up in her throat, and she forced it back down.

"All right, let's begin," Cascone said as she moved back into position in front of Yana and Sam.

"Since you didn't have a secret conversation with me, I don't know what I'm supposed to begin doing," Yana told her.

"You don't have to do anything," Cascone answered, a small smile tugging at her lips.

"Then how am—" Electricity shot through Yana's right hand before she could finish her question. Her eyes widened as she stared down at her fingers and realized she could see the bones glowing. Her skin became almost translucent, each vein becoming as clear as a river on a map. "Wh-wh-wh—" She couldn't get the whole word out. Her hand began to twitch, flopping back and forth like a dying fish. Yana pressed her left hand over her right, trying to keep it still. But it was as if her right hand was a hundred times stronger. It jerked away and shot into the air. Then it slapped her face—hard. She could feel the hot imprint of each finger on her cheek.

"Sam, that's not what I instructed you to do," Cascone said calmly.

Yana's hand fell back onto her lap, the glow disappearing as if a light switch under her skin had been flipped off. She stared at it for a moment until it started to feel like part of her own body again. Then she raised her gaze to Cascone. "What did you just say?"

Cascone didn't answer. She was too busy making a notation on her clipboard. Yana turned to Sam, meeting his dark eyes. "Did you just do that to me? Is that what she meant?"

Yana didn't wait for him to answer. *SLAP YOUR FACE.* The cracking sound his hand made when it hit his cheek made her grin. *No one hits me and gets away with it.* But the glow began in her fingers again. Her hand shot up, and she slapped herself again.

SLAP YOUR FACE! Sam obeyed her command, but her own hand was already moving into slapping position again.

"Enough!" Cascone barked. "Both of you."

Yana was able to lower her hand to her lap. She locked eyes with Sam. His eyes glittered with intensity, but she didn't look away. *He's the one who sent me the note warning me to say away from the Wilton Center,* she realized, her entire body going cold. *What does he know about this place?*

Rae lifted her hand to knock on Mandy's door. Before her fist touched the wood, the door flew open, and Mandy grabbed her by the wrist and pulled her inside. "What took you so long?" she exclaimed.

"I left the house two seconds after you called me," Rae answered. "Now, take a deep breath and tell me everything you saw."

"Emma and Zeke are eloping. I already told you that!" Mandy cried. "We've got to stop them. God, my dad's going to be home in half an hour. What am I supposed to tell him? How could Emma be such an idiot? Why—"

"Details. Did your vision give you any details?" Rae asked. "Come on. Let's sit down for a minute." She led the way to the living room.

"I can't sit down," Mandy answered. "My sister's eloping. *Eloping.* She's not even out of high school yet." She perched on the arm of the couch. "And

Zeke, I know you didn't find out that much about him, but he's going to ruin her life. I know it."

Should I slap her like they do in movies? Rae wondered. No. Somehow she didn't think it would work that well in real life. Mandy might start crying, and then Rae would never get any facts out of her. "So, in your vision Zeke and Emma were in his car, is that right?"

"Yeah. I told you that already." Mandy bounced up from the arm of the sofa and then immediately sat down next to Rae.

"Were there any street signs? Were they on the freeway? What were they driving by?" Rae tried to make her voice come out calm and firm. She hoped that would get an actual, helpful answer out of Mandy.

"Freeway. On 2," Mandy answered. "But that could go so many places. And I had to stop checking on them because my vision started to go and I wanted to recharge. So they could be anywhere! I need you to do your fingerprint thing on something of Emma's." Mandy was on her feet again, tugging at Rae's arm.

"Okay, okay, great plan. Let's do it," Rae said as Mandy propelled her down the hall. She flung open the bathroom door and pulled Rae inside.

"Use her electric razor. I know she was shaving

her legs before she left, probably trying to get all beautiful for her wedding to the scum bucket," Mandy said.

Rae grabbed a tissue and wiped the coat of wax off the fingers of her right hand. Gently she did a sweep of the razor.

/this is it/rice/when will I/am I/underwear/Zeke/

"Sorry, nothing," Rae told Mandy.

"Toothbrush next," Mandy ordered. "Emma's is the green one. Hurry. Hurry, hurry."

Please let me find something before a vessel bursts in Mandy's brain, Rae thought. Then she started a fresh sweep.

/wish I/no blood test/insane/something old/mom/mom/

"What next?" Rae asked Mandy.

"You didn't get anything?" Mandy wailed, like it was Rae's fault. "Do the moisturizer bottle." She started to tap her foot. Rae didn't think she'd ever seen anyone real do that before. She flexed her fingers a couple of times, then ran them over the bottle.

/tonight/birdseed/Ranburne/

Rae jerked her fingers away. "Ranburne. I think they're going to Ranburne. Which makes sense 'cause I got this info about no blood test, and I'm pretty sure Alabama doesn't make you take a blood test. It's right across the border."

"But where in Ranburne?" Mandy exclaimed. "We

need a chapel name. A street. Something. Otherwise Emma's going to be married before we get to her!"

At least following a bus is a no-brainer, Yana thought. No unexpected turns. No chance in hell it could outrun her little Bug. When the bus slowed down, Yana went on past it, then watched in her rearview as the passengers got off. No Sam.

So, lather, rinse, and repeat, she told herself. She took a trip around the block and put herself back behind the bus. At the next stop she passed the bus again and watched all the poor bus riders get off. "And there's my Sammy," she whispered. Yana pulled into the parking lot of a strip mall and watched Sam head down the sidewalk. The guy was a wreck. It looked like each step he took hurt him, even though he managed to keep up a decent pace.

When Sam turned a corner two blocks down, Yana gave him a couple of minutes head start, then she pulled on a floppy brown hat—her white-blond hair was what would get her noticed—and drove after him. It was harder following a pedestrian, especially on a nice residential street like the one Sam was heading down. There weren't a lot of cars, and if she went slow enough to stay behind Sam, he would definitely notice. She decided to pass him and park. Then she'd let him get another head start, follow on foot, and—

Yana grinned as she spotted Sam crossing a lawn toward a white house with light green shutters. "She shoots, she scores," Yana muttered. There'd be no awkward following-on-foot action today. She continued down the street, turned the corner, and found a parking space in front of another big house.

Time to see if Sam was just blowing smoke or if he actually had some useful info about the center. Yana climbed out of the Bug and walked back to Sam's house, taking her time. A girl out for a stroll, folks, nothing to worry about—that's the look she was shooting for. *Now, la-di-da, I'm just going to keep on strolling over to the back gate,* Yana thought as she walked over the soft grass. It had been cut recently, and the green smell of it filled her nose. She loved that smell.

Okay, now open the gate, she instructed herself. La-di-da again. She reached for the latch, and her whole body suddenly felt juiced. God, her hands were glowing again. Every rung of her spine was sizzling. Her hair was filled with static electricity. *Guess he knows I'm here,* she thought. Her legs and arms spasmed, and then she was climbing over the gate. She strained to get back control of her muscles, but she'd become a remote-controlled robot girl.

Is this what it feels like for them? she couldn't

help wondering. The people she thought-implanted, did they have this same horrible sense of being yanked by someone else's will? Like when she was controlling Rae, making her hurt herself, or when she'd almost had Anthony give Rae the—

Yana reached the top of the gate, then tumbled over, the fall pulling her out of her obsessive thoughts. When she landed, she found herself staring up at Sam. His loose, pale skin didn't look any better from this angle.

"You're an idiot," Sam told her. "You should be hundreds of miles away from here by now."

"Why? Because of your note?" Yana asked, relieved to be able to control her lips and jaw and tongue. She shoved herself to her feet. "It takes more than that to scare me."

"I repeat. You're an idiot," Sam said. He shoved his black hair off his face, and she saw that his forehead was dotted with sweat.

"I have reasons for being there," Yana replied.

"Your mother was in the group formed to boost psi powers. The agency killed her. Your genes got scrambled. You ended up with powers, too," Sam said matter-of-factly. "Now I'm guessing you're out for revenge. And you think that Cascone believes you're there just to refine your abilities. Which, by the way, she doesn't."

"How would Cascone—how did you—" Yana didn't know which question to ask first.

Sam raised an eyebrow at her. "You didn't think you were special, did you? *Mi problema es su problema.* Literally. And if you keep showing up at the center, you're going to end up exactly like me." He lowered himself to the grass and sat cross-legged.

"What is that supposed to mean?" Yana asked.

"I'm not talking to you if you're going to tower over me," Sam answered. He plucked a blade of grass and stuck it into his mouth.

"I thought only dogs ate grass," Yana commented as she sat down across from him.

Sam shrugged. "I like it. But maybe you have a sophisticated palate."

"So, okay, your mother was in the group with my mother—" Yana began.

"Try to keep up," Sam interrupted. "I think I already made that clear. And it's not like I have time to waste. I'm dying. You will be, too, unless you bolt. Even then they'll probably find you. But at least you'd have a two percent chance of survival."

"Dying." Yana picked up a piece of grass and stuck it in her own mouth. She needed something to do. Something besides look at him. Was he serious? He was around her age. And he was dying?

"Yeah, dying. As in decomposition bound. Getting ready for the dirt nap. Taking the—"

"I get it," Yana told him.

"Just wanted to make sure you did," he answered. "With you being slow and all. It's from all the experiments they did—radiation, electric impulses, a cornucopia of drugs. I thought at first it might be from using my power too much. I get spasms if I play Puppet Master a bunch of times in a row. But no. The side effects are basically harmless. I got that from stealing a look at the good doctor Kessler's notes. I'm dying because of all the games Cascone's been playing with my body."

"So why didn't you take off?" Yana demanded. "If you're so brilliant and all."

"I wanted to bring the bastards to their knees," Sam told her. "I kept waiting for my chance, waiting to find a way in. And they kept doing crap to me. I knew it was a race against time." He shrugged again. "I lost. So you can be like me. Or you can get out of town, get out of the country if you can."

"So you've given up?" Yana asked. If she were dying because of the agency, she'd want to bring it down even more.

"Of course, you might be the one they're looking for," Sam continued, ignoring her question. "If you are, they'll probably go all out keeping you alive. But the odds of that happening are worse than the odds of running and not getting caught."

What was he talking about? Was his brain being

eaten from the inside? "The one what?" Yana asked. She remembered the grass in her mouth and swallowed it. It tasted the way it smelled—green.

"I don't know, really. The one of us—the G-2s who ended up with powers from our moms—who can do *something.* I'm not sure exactly what." Sam plucked another blade of grass, put it between his lips, and blew, producing a high, thin whistle. "Tastes great and plays music."

Yana ate another piece of grass while she waited for her spinning mind to slow down again. She didn't know what she wanted to ask Sam first. "I don't get why you've given up. With what they've done to you, why don't you want to annihilate them?"

"Knowing you're dying, it changes the way you think." He started chewing his piece of grass. "Maybe the reason I like this stuff so much is because soon I'll be lying under it."

The green taste in Yana's mouth started to taste like rot. She turned her head and spit. The taste didn't go away.

Chapter 10

"We're about ten minutes outside of Ranburne," Anthony announced. "You ready to try getting a picture of Emma?" He glanced over his shoulder at Mandy. She had both hands knotted around the door handle, like she wanted to be ready to jump out at any second and run to her sister.

"Yeah. Okay, here goes," Mandy said. She reached out her hand, and Jesse handed her Emma's sweater.

"I wish I'd been able to get an exact location from one of Emma's fingerprints," Rae said softly. "I don't know how many more times Mandy's going to be able to use her power today."

"She's got something," Jesse called out.

Anthony checked the rearview mirror. Mandy was running her hands lightly down her face, her fingers barely touching her skin. It creeped him out to see her like that. All . . . empty. Mandy's face was blank. Her eyes like marbles, shiny and dead. He forced his attention back to the freeway. It wasn't going to help anyone if he slammed them all into the van up ahead.

Mandy let out a gurgling sigh. It sounded like a clogged drain emptying. Anthony risked another glance in the rearview mirror just as the life—the *Mandy*—came back into her face. "I was Emma. I was in a bathroom. I was pulling a wedding veil over my face," she told them. "I didn't see anything we can use. Nothing!"

"No, that's good—it means she's not married yet," Rae pointed out. "We're coming up to the first Ranburne exit. We'll get off there, go straight to a gas station and grab the yellow pages, and then we'll split up and each start—"

"It's going to be too late," Mandy interrupted. She started making a tiny braid in her long, light brown hair, the way she always did when she was freaking out about something.

"You don't know that," Anthony argued. Although the veil thing, that didn't sound good. He pulled into the exit lane, resisting the urge to floor the gas pedal.

What was the point of speed when you had no idea where you were going?

"You should try seeing her again," Jesse said. "She's probably out of the bathroom by now, right? If she was fixing her veil."

"Right. You're right," Mandy answered.

Jesse's a lifesaver, Anthony thought. Whenever he talked, Mandy calmed down a little. Focused more than she did when Anthony or Rae yammered at her.

"Any thoughts on direction here?" Anthony asked Rae as he came to a stop at the red light at the base of the exit ramp.

Rae took a look at Mandy. "Maybe you should pull over until she—"

"She's about to walk down the aisle," Mandy burst out. "I was looking at Zeke. He was standing next to a guy—a minister, I guess. Even though he didn't have on a robe or anything, just a suit. I was holding flowers in my hands. My heart, God, it was slamming against my ribs."

"Flowers," Jesse said. "Maybe that's something we can use. How many florists do you think are in this town?"

"Don't you get it? The wedding is happening now!" Mandy cried. "Right now! There's no time. Where's the sweater?"

"It's right in your lap," Jesse told her. "Is your vision going?"

Mandy didn't answer. She was gone again. The car behind Anthony gave a loud honk, and he realized he was sitting in front of a green light like a jerk. He turned right just to get out of the way.

"White Dove!" Mandy yelled. "There was a thing, a flyer, on the organ. It said White Dove."

Rae jerked out her cell phone and jammed in a few numbers. "In Ranburne. The White Dove chapel or church or anything close to that. I need an address."

"She was already in front of the minister. He was doing the dearly beloved part," Mandy exclaimed, her voice coming out high and breathy.

"Jesse, she's starting to hyperventilate. Make her put her head between her knees," Anthony ordered.

"1413 Trona Way," Rae repeated.

Anthony rolled down his window and slowed down a little so he was even with the car in the next lane. "Do you know where Trona Way is?" he shouted. No one in the other car even glanced at him. *Because their windows are up, moron,* Anthony thought. He gave three quick blasts on the horn, and the woman in the passenger seat turned her head toward him. He made a roll-down-your-window gesture, and a second later her window was sliding down. "Do you know where Trona Way is?" he shouted again.

"Trona Way?" she shouted back.

"Yes!" Rae, Jesse, and Anthony yelled.

The woman turned toward the driver. "Does she live in this place or not?" Jesse muttered. "Just keep breathing, Mandy. But not so fast," he added.

The woman turned back around. "Make a left, then a right," she called.

"Thank you!" Rae yelled. "Thanks so much."

Anthony pulled into the left lane just in time to hit another red light. "Crap!"

"What's wrong?" Mandy asked, her voice coming out muffled because her face was still pressed between her knees.

"Nothing," Anthony told her. "A red light. Nothing." *Change,* he mentally ordered the light. *Change now.* It didn't. Why would it? It wasn't like he had any freakin' psychic powers. He locked his eyes on the light. A few seconds later it went green. Anthony made the turn and immediately pulled into the right lane. *At least I don't have to wait for the light this time,* he thought as he made the turn.

"There it is! Trona." Rae slid closer to him and wrapped her fist in the side of his T-shirt. He loved the way she always did that—like he could make her feel safe. If only he could actually *keep* her safe.

"Get ready to look at the numbers," he instructed, pushing away the nagging thought about what Yana was up to. "I'm going right, but I don't know if it's the right way." He made the turn.

"That one's thirteen twenty-seven," Jesse said.

"We're going the wrong way," Rae announced. "I see thirteen twenty-five."

Anthony did a traffic check, then a cop check. Nothing. He made a screeching U-turn. "It should be on my side of the street," Rae told him. He nodded and pulled into the right lane.

"We're almost there, Mandy," Jesse said. "I can see it from here. See it, Anthony? See the signs with the birds?"

"Got it," Anthony answered. He floored the gas, went through a yellow light, then double-parked in front of the chapel. *Is this totally insane?* he wondered as he jumped out of the car and led the charge to the main doors. *Maybe Emma and what's-his-name* should *be getting married.*

Mandy darted ahead of him and pushed open the doors. "Emma!" she shouted.

"There's a wedding going on in there," a woman in a white suit snapped.

"I know!" Mandy snapped back. "Emma!" she shouted again. Then she burst through the double wooden doors on the left. Anthony went after her, feeling like an idiot as he, Jesse, and Rae followed Mandy down the aisle with the minister, Emma, and Zeke—that was his name—staring at them.

"Did you do it already?" Mandy demanded.

The printer stopped, and silence filled Sam's bedroom. He rolled his desk chair over, retrieved the freshly printed sheaf of paper, stuck one of those clamps on the top, rolled back to Yana, and handed it to her. "This is everything I've been able to find out about the agency."

"What are all these maps?" Yana asked, flipping through the pages.

"Most of them show locations of the other G-2s," Sam answered. "I don't think it'll be too long before they're rounded up. Poor bastards."

"Rounded up?" Yana repeated. *Rae,* she thought. The name screamed through her head. Was something going to happen to Rae?

"Yeah, you and me, we're just guinea pigs since we were stupid enough to walk into the agency and volunteer," Sam told her. He twisted back and forth in the swivel chair, then spun himself completely around. "But it seems that they've perfected the N-Tetran. Or perhaps it would be more fair to say that *I* perfected it since I'm the lucky, lucky boy who got to try out all the earlier versions." Sam did another spin.

"N-Tetran?" Yana said.

"The drug you got to sample today," Sam answered. "I heard from my good friend Dr. Kessler how well it worked. Cascone's kept the development of N-Tetran a secret from everybody. Control is very important to our Layla Cascone. I suspect she didn't want to inform her superiors until she could give them a drug guaranteed effective. By tomorrow or the next day at the latest, I'm sure that one of the samples they have left will be being analyzed in a lab. Then it will be produced in larger quantities. And they'll need lots of G-2s to test it on. There are going to be families all over the country reporting their teenagers missing. The police'll probably never put it together. Teen runaways are too common."

"Cascone's going to keep them—us—prisoner. Is that what you're saying?" Yana demanded, her throat getting tight. Two words repeated in her brain. Rae. Mandy. Rae. Mandy. And so many others . . .

"Now that they've figured out how to boost our powers, yeah. It wouldn't be safe for humanity to have all of us wandering free—not unless they could all be fitted with blocks," Sam answered. "And once we have boosted powers, I'm sure they'll find tasks for everybody, not just the one, whoever that turns out to be. Of course, I'll be dead, so . . ." Sam shrugged.

"That's it? You'll be dead, so screw the rest of us?" Yana muttered. She sat down on Sam's bed, and the guy actually blushed. *I bet I'm the first girl who's ever set foot in his bedroom,* she thought. *And probably the last,* she couldn't stop herself from adding.

"Cascone and company, as I'm sure you figured out, found a way to block our powers," Sam answered. "If they hadn't—" He shrugged. "Well, let's just say things would be a lot different."

"So you gave up just because you couldn't use your powers?" Yana demanded. "It's not like powers are the only way to deal with people. I'm thinking a big can of gasoline and some matches. I'm thinking tonight, while they still think I'm a good little guinea pig. The center can burn, can't it?"

"I don't see why not," Sam answered. "But you'll get caught, you know."

Yana felt like she had a volcano in her chest. Seething, bubbling. Ready to erupt. "So what they did to our moms, that's okay. Just, oh, well." She shrugged, the way Sam had about forty times since she'd met him. "And what about all those other G-2s who are going to get yanked from their homes? What about them? My friend Rae's dad, I don't think he'd survive if she disappeared, but—" She shrugged again.

"Agency very big. Guinea pig very small," Sam answered. "Guinea pig fight agency. Guinea pig end up splotch on ground." He stood up and stepped closer to her, close enough for her to smell the decay, the stench of his sick body rotting. "Did I make it simple enough for you to understand, Yana?" he asked quietly.

She looked away, not wanting him to see any pity in her eyes. "Gas. Match. Tonight. That's even simpler. Worst-case scenario, I can destroy the N-Tetran samples. That'll slow Cascone down, at least. And best-case scenario, I can do a lot more than that," she told him. "You could come with me. For your mom. For all of us."

"I'm trying to keep breathing until Christmas. My dad's big on Christmas," Sam answered. "In case you need it more plainly, that means I'm out."

Yana turned and headed for the door without another word. What else was there to say? As she reached for the doorknob, something hit her back and then dropped to the floor. She turned around and saw a plastic bag of . . . she wasn't sure what. They looked kind of like silver buttons.

"Stick them on the security cameras. It'll scramble the signal," Sam said. "Of course, when they start seeing static on the monitors, they're going to start checking the place out. They'll probably figure out someone's broken in, but they won't know exactly where you are."

Yana knelt down and picked up the bag. "Thanks."

"You shouldn't be thanking me. You should be forgetting your whole insane plan," Sam told her. He shrugged. "But since you're not, I suppose you'd like the security codes for the doors, too."

"What are you doing here?" Emma cried, throwing up the veil that had been covering her face. "Have you been spying on me? Did you tell Dad that—"

"Did you do it already?" Mandy asked again. "Did you actually marry . . . *that?*" She flicked her fingers at Zeke.

Probably not the way to go, Mandy, Rae thought. Emma at least thought she loved the guy. It was only going to make her angrier to hear Mandy badmouth him.

"Who are all of you?" the minister asked, his gaze flicking from Mandy to Rae to Anthony to Jesse, then back to Mandy.

"I'm her sister." Mandy pointed at Emma. "What are you doing letting her get married? She's still in high school."

"I'm eighteen," Emma protested. She turned to the minister. "I showed you proof. So did Zeke. And we paid our money. She—" Emma jerked her head toward Mandy "—doesn't have any say in whether we get married or not."

"Emma, you don't want to be doing this," Mandy pleaded, her voice cracking with emotion. "What about UCLA? What about all your plans?"

"Plans change, Mandy," Emma said. "Look, you're here. Why don't you sit down and watch me get married and be happy for me?"

Rae glanced at Zeke. He had the same blank stare he'd had at the music store—eyes glazed over, no visible emotion. It was like the Mandy-Emma drama was something he was watching on TV. *Is he stoned right now?* she wondered. *At his own wedding?*

"I can't be happy for you," Mandy answered. "You can't expect me to be happy for you when you're throwing away your life." She paused, and Rae could tell she was struggling over her next words. Suddenly Rae knew what they would be. "Em, do you think Mom would be happy for you?" Mandy asked softly.

Tears filled Emma's eyes. "How can you bring up Mom? This is supposed to be my best day ever." She turned toward the minister, her back to Mandy. "Please keep going. We were almost to the part with the rings."

The minister's answer came too softly for Rae to hear. Mandy shot Rae a pleading look. *What does she want me to do?* Rae thought. *What* can *I do? I barely know Emma. Or Zeke. Why would they listen to me?*

"Rae," Anthony whispered, his breath warm against his ear. "Two o'clock?"

"What?" she whispered back.

"I must ask everyone but our witnesses to leave the chapel," the minister announced, his voice gentle but firm.

"Fingerprint stuff, in the pew up ahead to the left," Anthony explained. "Maybe you can—"

"Yeah. Maybe," Rae answered, understanding him without needing to hear all the words, the way she so often did. "Try to buy me a little time." She hurried forward and slipped into the pew.

"Mandy, I think you should stay," Anthony said loudly. "I think you'll end up wishing you'd seen your sister get married."

Rae tuned out all the voices speaking around her. She ran her naked fingers over the straps of Emma's purse—

/get away/dress/love him/UCLA/start my life/bridesmaids/forever/gotta pee/what job will/forever/

—and the buttons and collar of Zeke's jean jacket.

/before she'll do it/smarter/get some/college guy/kids/don't want kids/

Hope I got enough, Rae thought. She stood up. Anthony had somehow gotten Mandy and Jesse seated in a pew. Emma was just about to pull her veil back over her face.

"Emma, um, I know that we hardly know each other," Rae began. "And there's no reason you should listen to me. But, uh, my sister got married when she was around your age." Big lie. Good cause. "It didn't end up that great. It turned out that she wanted kids and the guy didn't and they'd never even talked to each other about it. And he was assuming that she'd live with him on campus at, uh, Columbia, but she didn't want to leave California at all. But you guys, you two, have probably talked about all that, right?"

"We don't need to talk about every tiny thing," Emma answered. She reached out and took Zeke's hand. "We're in love. We want the same things."

"Like kids?" Rae pressed. She'd gotten a lot of anxiety off Zeke's thought about kids.

"We definitely want kids," Emma said.

Zeke didn't contradict her, but Rae thought she saw a flicker of panic in his eyes. Genuine feeling for the first time.

"Good, that's good," Rae went on. "Because marriage . . . it's forever, right?" She looked at the minister, who nodded. "And that's a long time."

Forever was the thing that Emma seemed the most agitated about. That and the bridesmaids and dress thoughts. "And since it's forever, and you're only getting married once, don't you guys want the whole deal—the dress, the bridesmaids? God, you won't even have any pictures for a wedding album."

"We'll have a big wedding later, with all our friends. And family," Emma said, talking directly to Mandy.

"Who's going to pay for that?" Zeke asked.

"We will," Emma answered. "I'm going to be working full-time now—"

"You're not going to find a job that'll pay you that kind of money," Zeke protested.

"If I went to college, I—" Emma began.

Knew you still wanted to go. Knew you didn't want to drop out, Rae thought. She smiled at Mandy, and Mandy smiled back.

"We talked about that," Zeke interrupted. "There's no money for college, either. That's why we decided there was no point in you staying in school."

Emma pulled her hand out of Zeke's. "If we asked my dad, if we could live with him until—"

"No way. No way can we be having sex with your dad across the hall," Zeke told her.

"And her sister," Mandy piped up.

"God. That's all you ever think about," Emma accused him, her cheeks flushing a deep pink. "It's like it's all you want me for."

Keep going, you guys. Keep on going, Rae thought.

Chapter 11

Yana put on her Happy Burger uniform, complete with its Have a Happy Happy Burger Day pin and the dorky little cloth visor. She studied herself in the mirror inside her closet door. "Just a happy, happy Happy Burger delivery girl," she told her reflection, then she picked up a big cardboard box with smiling lips all over it, one of the ones used for delivering big orders. There were no burgers or fries inside it, though. Just big bottles of lighter fluid. "We are happy to offer free delivery anywhere in Atlanta." She plastered a happy smile on her face. It looked fake—fake and scared—to her, but she thought it would work on the upstairs security guard at the Wilton Center.

She closed the closet door and glanced around

her room. The bed was made. Her clothes were put away. Her desk was organized. *It looks like nobody lives here,* she thought. But that was how it always looked. That's how she liked it. When she was younger—actually not that much younger, like a couple of weeks ago younger—she used to imagine it was a hotel room. She'd lie in her bed, making up stories about the city she was sleeping in that night. Was she ever going to see her room again?

Don't even go there, Yana ordered herself. She checked the clock. God, she was ready way too early. Why had she thought it would take this long to buy some squirt bottles of lighter fluid and get dressed? She wished she could just go now. She'd been waiting so long. Almost five years.

But she had to wait a little longer. Her plan depended on going in at precisely the right time. If she went now, there'd still be people in the classes held at the center, people who had no clue they were helping out the agency by giving the center the appearance of a normal place where normal classes were taught. Those people, doing their knitting and flamenco dancing and meditation, they all needed time to finish up and get out of the center. That meant she had to wait an hour and—she checked the clock again—an hour and thirteen minutes, which would give them time to gather their stuff and go to the bathroom and chat with their friends and still be on their way to their safe little homes before Yana pulled in the center's parking lot.

Yana checked the clock again, even though she knew not even a minute had passed. She had to be careful not to wait *too* long. Cascone usually worked late. So did some of the other doctors. When Yana went in, she wanted them to be there. Torching the building would destroy some research, and she'd make sure she got rid of all the N-Tetran samples. That would slow things down. Buy some time for Rae and Mandy and the other G-2s. But if she wanted to really damage the agency, she had to make her move while at least some of the people in charge were in the building.

She sat down on the edge of her bed, careful not to mess up the comforter, and rested her cheek against the cardboard box she held cradled in her arms. Her eyes followed the second hand around the face of the clock. Again, and again, and again.

Soon, she thought. *Soon, soon, soon.*

I guess I'd call this mission accomplished, Anthony thought. Mandy's sister was crying and yelling. Zeke was yelling back. Anthony definitely didn't think there was going to be a wedding today. Or anytime soon.

The shouting was giving him a freakin' headache, and he really didn't want to get all caught up in some other family's melodrama—he got enough of that at home—so he headed out of the chapel, wandered over to his car, and sat on the hood. He closed his eyes, tilted back his head, and let the sun warm his face.

"Hey, you."

Anthony opened his eyes and saw Rae standing in front of him. "Hey." He shoved his hair off his face. "So is it under control in there?"

"I think so," Rae answered. "Mandy and Jesse have Emma in—" She was interrupted by the sound of the chapel door being slammed shut. Zeke stalked out, climbed in a battered Chevy Nova, and peeled off, tires screeching. "Yeah, I'd definitely say our work here is through," Rae said, watching Zeke's car turn the corner and disappear.

"I guess I should move into his spot. Lucky I didn't get a ticket for double-parking already." Anthony climbed in the Hyundai, and Rae got in beside him. He maneuvered the car into the spot, then turned off the engine.

"It's probably going to be a little while before Emma pulls herself together," Rae told him.

Anthony nodded. He didn't care how long she took. Hanging out in the car with Rae was one of his favorite things. It was like the inside of the car was a whole separate world, and he and Rae were the only two people who existed.

"Thanks for doing this." Rae reached over, took his arm, and pulled it around her shoulders.

"No prob," Anthony answered, tracing little circles on the top of her arm with his thumb. "I thought maybe Mandy was freaking out over nothing, but it seems like neither one of them really wanted to get married."

"Yeah," Rae said. "That was pretty clear when I did the fingerprint sweep."

Anthony gave a laugh that came out sounding more like a bark. "Can you imagine what your dad would do if he thought the two of us were getting married?"

"With both of us still in high school? He'd go—" Rae stopped abruptly and stared at him. "But that's not what you meant, is it? You meant if we wanted to get married *ever*, right?"

She sounded pissed. What did he say?

"Anthony, do you even—I mean, I *love* you."

Anthony blinked back at her, trying to process what to feel. Had she just said what he thought she'd said? But then, why did she still sound angry?

"I love you," she repeated, erasing any doubt that he'd heard her wrong. "Do you think I would love someone who was a big loser? 'Cause that's what you think you are, right? Somebody my dad wouldn't ever want me to be with."

Anthony felt like he'd been zapped with a stun gun. Rae loved him. Rae Voight actually loved *him.* He gave his head a slight shake as he realized what else she'd said. "Come on, like your dad doesn't want you to marry some college guy," he said, but his voice came out a little funny. He didn't even know how to react to that other part.

"First, you could be some college guy if you wanted to," Rae answered. "Second, my dad would want me to be with someone who . . . God, who was *good* to me, someone who'd be there for me. The way you always have been."

"Yeah, I guess," he admitted.

"You guess?" Rae's voice rose higher. "Anthony, Marcus is going to be some college guy. Do you think my dad would want me to be with him? Do you think *I'd* want to be with anyone like him? Someone who's such a weenie that he cares more about what other people think than about me?"

"He is a weenie," Anthony agreed.

"And I shouldn't be with a weenie, right?" Rae asked.

"No. You definitely shouldn't be with a weenie," he answered.

"And would you call yourself a weenie?" Rae asked. She slid closer to him until her face was about an inch away from his.

"No." Anthony couldn't stop a smile from spreading across his face, a smile so big, it hurt.

Then, slowly, he felt the smile fade. His throat closed up until it was the size of one of those straws they put in drinks at bars. There was something he had to say to her. Now. But he didn't know if he could.

"Rae . . ."

His heart started to flail around, like it wanted to get out of his chest. This was so friggin' hard. What if she laughed? Or said she'd only been kidding when she said it to him? Or—

"Rae," he began again. He pulled in a deep breath, hoping it would open up his throat a little. "Rae, I love you, too."

She closed the fraction of space between them and kissed him, a light, sweet kiss that he felt in every square inch of his body.

"I love you," he said again, without letting his lips break contact with hers. And that time it was easy, the easiest thing he'd ever said.

It's finally time, Yana thought. *It's finally time, Mom.* She stepped out of her Bug, her big cardboard

Happy Burger box in her arms, and used her butt to slam the car door. She slapped the smile she'd rehearsed in her bedroom on her face and headed to the main doors. They were unlocked. A good sign, she told herself as she walked inside and turned down the hall that led to the room with the security monitors.

The security guard popped his head out of the room before she was even halfway there. "Got a food order," Yana called. "A big one." She nodded toward the box in her arms. "You must be having a party."

The guard ran his hand over his short, bristly hair. "Let me call downstairs and check."

"No!" Yana exclaimed. "The guy who called in the order said upstairs, turn right when you get in the door. Maybe I just got the address wrong." She kept talking as she walked toward him, trying to keep him away from the phone. "God, if I screwed up, my boss is going to be pissed. All the food will be cold and—" Yana reached the guard and put down the box. "I'll have to go back and get a whole new order."

She kept her eyes on the guard's face so she wouldn't somehow signal what she was going to do as she reached into her pocket and slid out the stun gun. She couldn't risk using her thought-implanting ability on this guy. Who knew if he had the same power to block her as the others downstairs? "I hope I don't get fired," she said. Then she zapped the guy. He didn't even see it coming. He stared up at her, unable to move. Yana pulled a roll of duct tape out of her other pocket and taped his mouth closed, then taped his feet together; then she hauled him over onto his stomach and taped his hands together behind his back. Breathing hard from the effort, she managed to drag him back into his little room.

The guard was giving angry little sounds of protest behind his tape gag, and the grunts made Yana's stomach turn over. She was leaving a helpless man up here. When the fire—Yana shook her head hard, trying to send the thought flying out of her brain. "You knew exactly what was going on downstairs. You knew. You should have gone to work at the 7-Eleven." She stepped outside, shut the door firmly behind her, and picked up her box.

Everyone who is left in here deserves what they're going to get, she reminded herself as she sprinted down the hall, the metal lighter fluid cans banging around inside the box. *All the innocent people are on their way home or already there, settled in front of the tube.*

Yana slid to a halt in front of the first camera, the one a few feet away from the door leading to the basement door. It was bolted to the wall above her head. She dropped the box, then climbed up on it, pulled one of the scrambling devices out of the plastic bag in her bra, and stuck it on the camera. The scrambler had a magnet on it to hold it in place. Sam had thought of everything.

You can tell him thanks when this is over, she told herself as she jumped off the box and picked it up again. *For now just move. Move, move, move!* With three long strides she reached the door to the stairs. She raised one knee and used it to balance the box while she punched in the security code and opened the door. She hesitated for a moment, listening. She didn't hear any footsteps on the stairs.

So move! she thought. She started down the stairway, moving as fast as she could with the box. She heard the sound of metal slamming against wood. Crap. That was the door at the bottom of the flights of stairs. Yana backed up a few stairs so that she was about halfway above the landing between the first two flights. She could hear footsteps racing toward her. A second later two guards rounded the landing and started up the flight below her.

"I give up!" Yana shouted. The guards didn't slow down. *Let them come, let them come,* she instructed herself. They hit the landing directly below her. Yana tossed the box over the stair railing to the flight of stairs a level down. Then she grabbed the railing with both hands and vaulted over. *Now I'm ahead of them, at least,* she thought as she snatched up the box and started to run. Not very far ahead of them, though. They'd already turned around. They were coming after her. The sound of their boots on the cement stairs was like thunder.

Yana rounded the second landing. She could see the door to the basement. Five, seven, three, one, one, five, two, she chanted. She slammed to a stop in front of the door and started punching in the code. The guards had reached the last flight, too. She could hear them. In another second they'd be able to—

The door opened. Yana bolted inside. She spun toward the keypad on her side of the door and started hitting a new combination of numbers. *Faster, faster,* she thought. She could hear the guards yelling. They were right on the other side of the door.

But they were too late. Yana punched in the last two numbers she needed to change the code. Thanks again, Sam. Now no one could get in without the new code—her code. And no one could get out.

Don't stand around congratulating yourself. There are security monitors down here, too. Yana scanned the front hall and spotted a camera to her left. She darted over, dropped the box, jumped up on it, and placed a scrambler. In the distance she heard voices. She thought one was Cascone's. Yana ran in the opposite direction. Out of the corner of her eye she caught sight of a metal box on one wall. Score. The fuse box. She opened it and used the side of her hand to click off a whole row of switches at once. When she shut off the second row, the hallway she stood in went dark.

The voices were coming closer. Yana ducked into the closest room. Crap. It was small, with just a desk and a chair. Not much of a place to hide. She jammed her box under the desk, then positioned herself to one side of the door and got her stun gun ready, just in case. *Maybe they won't even look in here,* she thought.

But a moment later the door swung open. Yana stood motionless, crammed between the door and the wall. She wasn't going to use the stun gun unless she had to. Whoever was out there would make a sound falling to the floor. They might even have time to yell before Yana got their mouth taped. And that would give away her location.

How long can it take to check a tiny office? she wondered. Had whoever was out there spotted her box? Had they already seen her but didn't want her to know they had? Her heart began to beat so hard that she could feel her pulse in her temples, in her throat, even in her fingers.

Footsteps moved toward her, soft on the carpeted floor. *How can they not hear my heart?* she wondered. It was thudding so loudly, she was surprised the floor wasn't vibrating.

The door swung away from Yana, taking with it her hiding place. She raised the stun gun—but she was alone. The person searching the room had gone, shutting the door behind them.

Don't move. Not yet, Yana thought. She held herself so still that her muscles screamed in protest. For a minute. Two. *Okay, they should be finished with this hallway,* she decided. She stepped away from the wall and hurried over to the desk, knelt down, and pulled out her box. She removed one of the cans of lighter fluid and doused the carpet, the sharp smell of the gas filling her nose, her mouth, her lungs.

"If I'm going to do this, I'm going to do it right," Yana whispered. She opened the desk's file drawer and started emptying the files onto the floor. She made a big pile under the wooden desk.

It wasn't time to start lighting matches. Not yet. She had more gas to pour. And she had to find the N-Tetran samples. But when it was time, this room would make quite a bonfire. Yana took a backpack out of the box and slid three cans of lighter fluid inside, then put the backpack on. She grabbed the last two cans of fluid, then headed for the door and opened it a few inches.

She could hear voices, close, but not too close. She slipped out into the hallway and started toward the next door, leaving a trail of lighter fluid behind her as she walked. *For you, Mom. And for you, Sam. And for you, Rae. And for your mother. And for Mandy and her mother. And for Sam's mother. For all of us.*

Chapter 12

I can't believe he actually said he loved me, Rae thought for the millionth time. They'd driven all the way back to Atlanta, and she was still reliving that moment. It wasn't that she hadn't thought he loved her. The way he looked at her, the things he did for her. God, he'd stood guard over her while she slept. But she hadn't thought he'd actually say the words. It just didn't seem like an Anthony thing to do. She glanced over at him, and her mouth curved into a smile. That's what looking at him did to her. The least of what it did to her.

"What?" Anthony asked.

"Nothing," Rae answered. *It's just that you said you love me.* She felt like rolling down the window and yelling it to every car they passed. *Anthony told me he loved me! Anthony told me he loved me!*

But with Emma in the backseat, breathing in that way you breathe when you're trying not to cry, shouting about how much Anthony loved Rae wouldn't exactly be thoughtful. Neither was yelling about how much Rae loved Anthony, which was the other thing she felt like shouting to every person in every car.

Rae twisted around and caught Mandy's eye. "How are you guys doing back there?" she asked.

"I can't believe I was almost married," Emma said, staring down at her lap. "Married. I was only a few words from being married."

"But you're not," Mandy told her. "It's okay."

Emma scrubbed her face with her hands. "And Zeke. I don't know if I'll ever even see him again."

"Do you want to?" Jesse asked, sounding vaguely disgusted. Clearly he was in the Mandy zone—whatever she thought, he thought.

"I don't know," Emma answered. She wrapped her arms around herself. But her own arms weren't strong enough to stop the shudders running through her body.

"Almost home," Anthony announced as he turned onto Mandy and Emma's street.

"Stop here, okay?" Emma asked. "I need to talk to Becky."

"Her best friend," Mandy explained. "From when they used to walk to kindergarten together."

Anthony pulled over. "You want me to come in with you?" Mandy asked. She didn't want to let her sister out of her sight. Rae could see that.

"No," Emma said sharply. She opened the car door and started to climb out. Then she turned back and gave Mandy a hard hug. "Thank you." She got out and slammed the door before Mandy could answer. *Did she see it on Mandy's face?* Rae wondered. *Could she see how worried Mandy was? How much Mandy loves her?*

"Hey, let's go to Chick Filet or someplace," Jesse said. "I'm starving." *And you're not ready to end your Mandy time,* Rae thought.

Anthony shot Rae a look that had a question in it. She nodded. Yeah, she'd rather drop Mandy and Jesse off at their homes. She was dying to have Anthony all to herself. But how could she stand in the way of the sweet thing that was starting up between Mandy and Jesse?

"You mind if I wear your sweatshirt, Anthony?" Mandy asked as he made a U-turn. She grabbed it off the floor without waiting for an answer, and her face drained of animation. She began twisting her hands in her lap.

"She's gone," Jesse said, his voice cracking.

"Pull over," Mandy croaked. "I have to throw up."

Anthony changed lanes and pulled over to the curb. Mandy clambered out of the car. Rae got out, too, and held Mandy's long hair back while she vomited, vomited until everything in her was gone and her body shook with dry heaves.

"Here." Anthony leaned out the passenger window and handed Rae a Coke. "It's warm, but—"

"Perfect," Rae said. She popped the top, ignoring the concerned Anthony thoughts she was picking up, and handed the can to Mandy. "Drink this."

Mandy sucked down half the can, wiped her mouth with her arm, and turned to Rae. "I saw Yana," she whispered. "She was gagging on fumes. Gas, I think."

"Where was she?" Rae cried.

"I don't know," Mandy burst out.

Anthony leaned out the window. "I forgot that Yana wore that sweatshirt the last time she was in the car. Are you okay, Mandy?"

"Do you think you can look again? Will you be all right?" Rae asked.

"Yeah. My vision's getting a little blurry. It hasn't been long enough since the last time. But yeah," Mandy answered. She wiped her mouth again. Then she handed Rae the sweatshirt and immediately took it back, squeezing it tightly to make the connection.

An instant later Mandy's face went blank. Then she gasped, a sound that made Rae's stomach try to crawl out of her body. Slowly Mandy raised her arms.

Like she's surrendering to someone, Rae thought. *God, what's happening to Yana?*

Mandy blinked rapidly, then met Rae's eyes. "She was starting a fire in a trash can. I don't know where. A place with no windows. And two men—in uniforms—came at her. Rae, they were pointing guns at her. I think they're going to kill her."

"Get back in the car," Rae ordered as she jumped back in the front seat. "We have to go to the Wilton Center. Yana's in trouble."

"You caught me, okay?" Yana said, keeping her hands high but refusing to loosen her grip on the handles of the two metal boxes she'd found in the lab. The N-Tetran samples were staying with her. "Take me to Cascone. I know she'll want to see me right away."

The fire she'd lit in the trash can jumped to the trail of lighter fluid she'd splashed through the basement. Neither guard took his eyes off her. She heard a click, then another. *It's the safeties on the guns going off. They're going to kill me. Right here. Right now.*

Yana wanted to bolt. At least make them have to hit a moving target. But her feet felt like they had melded to the floor. The flames were scorching the skin of her right leg, but even that wasn't enough to get her muscles to obey her screaming brain. "Do you two even know who you're guarding?" she burst out. "My mother was murdered by—"

The hands of the guard on the left began to glow. He threw his gun behind him, his mouth dropping open in astonishment.

"What in the hell did you—" the other guard began. Then his hands began to glow, showing the bones and veins. An instant later he threw his gun behind him.

"Now would be the time to run," a voice said from behind Yana. She snapped her head toward the sound and saw Sam standing there.

"How . . . You can't be here. I changed the codes," Yana cried.

"You don't think I taught you *every* trick I know, do you?" Sam yelled back. "Move! Now!"

Yana's body jerked, and she was free. She raced toward Sam, the metal boxes bouncing against her legs. He grabbed her by the wrist and pulled her to the left. "There's another set of stairs," he told her as they ran. They rounded the corner—and saw a wall of fire. Yana's hair crackled, and her eyes burned even though she and Sam were several feet away from it.

"Back the way we came," she barked. This time Yana took the lead, pulling Sam with her. A chunk of sizzling plaster bounced off her shoulder. She looked up and saw that the fire had begun eating the ceiling.

"I can't even see the end of the hallway," Sam cried. Neither could Yana. The smoke was too thick. It felt as heavy as bricks as it invaded her mouth and nose and thudded down her throat into her lungs.

"Get down," Yana instructed. She hit the floor, pulling Sam down beside her, and started army-crawling forward, the metal boxes clanging. "I'm keeping one foot against the wall. When we get to the T-section of the hall, we go right."

"Okay. I'll follow you," Sam answered, his voice weak and raspy.

Yana kept crawling. So slow. She was moving way too slow. But she was afraid if she stood up, she'd pass out. *So don't stand up,* she told herself. *Who cares if it's slow? As long as you keep going.*

Left elbow. Clang as one of the metal boxes hit the floor. Right knee. Right elbow. Clang as the other metal box hit the floor. Left knee. Again. Again. Again. At least no guards were looking for them. She could hear shouts and footsteps, but as far as she could tell, everyone was only thinking about finding a way out. Left elbow. Clang. Right knee. Right elbow. Clang. Left knee. Again. Again. Again. Should they have reached the T-section by now? Could she have missed it? "Sam, we didn't go past the opening, did we?" Yana called.

He didn't answer. "Sam!" Yana shouted. She peered through the smoke. Her eyes were stinging so badly, she almost couldn't see. She reached out her hand and groped along the floor, keeping the handle of the metal box looped over her thumb. Where was he? "Sam!" she shouted again. She used her hands to push herself backward along the linoleum floor. Every few feet she swept her arm to the side, reaching for him, feeling for him. Where was he? *Where was he?*

Yana shinnied backward another few feet. Reached out and felt flesh beneath her fingers. She wriggled closer and saw that her hand was on Sam's arm. He lay there, motionless. "Keep moving! You don't want to die in here!" She shoved him hard. His body slid limply across the floor. "Sam! Wake up! Come on! Wake! Up!"

She heard him pull in a shaky breath, a breath that rattled up from deep in his chest. "Yes. That's it. You've got to keep breathing." Yana wrapped her arm around his shoulders and started to crawl forward again. She was sure the metal box was cutting into his skin, but who cared about that? Left elbow. Clang. Right knee. Drag Sam forward with right arm. Left knee. "You don't have to do anything but breathe," she choked out. "I'll do the rest." She reached out and felt for the wall with her toe. They weren't to the T-section of the hall yet. At least she didn't think so. She kept crawling. Dragging. Checking with her toe. Checking with her toe until the wall wasn't there anymore.

"Now we just go right and then we're to the stairs," she told Sam. He didn't answer. She wasn't sure if he was even breathing anymore. And she didn't want to find out for sure. Not until she got him out of here. Out of the smoke and heat. Once she did that, he'd be okay.

Yana kept crawling. Her lungs felt like they were on fire themselves. Every breath she managed to pull in made the fire in them hotter. *Keep going,* she told herself. *Keep going. You have to get out. You can't let them win. For Mom.* Left elbow. Clang. *For Rae.* Right knee. *For Sam.* She dragged Sam forward with her left arm. *For Mandy.* Left elbow.

Wait. Her elbow had hit something. Yana explored with her fingers, her thumb cramping as she tightened it around the handle of the metal box. Her fingers hit flesh again. Blistered flesh. Hot bile hit the back of her throat. *Don't think about it now,* she told herself. *You've got to keep going.* But she couldn't crawl over the . . . the body. Not dragging Sam. She was going to have to stand up and carry him.

Yana staggered to her feet. And saw a tiny red light blinking through the smoke. The keypad for the door. The . . . body must have been trying to reach the door. *Don't think about it now,* she told herself again. She brought her face as close to the keypad as she could, and the numbers came into focus. She punched in the new code, the metal keys burning her finger with each touch.

"Did it," she muttered when the door clicked open. "We're outta here, Sam." Yana bent down and hauled Sam to his feet. She wrapped his arm around her shoulders and held it in place with one hand. Then she started up the stairs.

Her shoulder muscles screamed in protest, but Yana didn't let go of Sam. Didn't let go of the boxes. Right foot. Left foot. Up, up, up. "We're almost halfway there, Sam," she said. It wasn't true. They were only halfway up the first flight, and there was still another flight left to go. But Sam wasn't looking.

Yana hauled in a deep breath. Better. The air was so much cooler out here. She sucked in another breath. It was like a fire hose had been turned on her lungs. Energy flooded her body. She started taking the steps two at a time. Sam's feet were barely touching the floor. But he didn't feel heavy. It was like she'd become a superhero or something. Like if she had to lift a car off a kid right now, she could do it. Left foot. Right foot. Left foot. Right foot. Leftrightleftrightleftright.

And here was the door. Yana shoved it open. The air in the hallway of the first floor was even better. "Just a little ways more, Sam." Yana bent down and looped one of her arms under his knees. She'd carry him the rest of the way. He was light, probably because he was sick. And she was flying, flying for the main exit. She bet she was pumping more adrenaline right that second than she had in the rest of her life combined. "Yeah!" Yana screeched as she shoved open the big double doors and burst out into the night air. "We did it! We did it, Sam!" The adrenaline drained out of her body, leaving her limp. She gently lowered Sam to the ground. She'd just rest for a sec—

A horrible sound filled her ears. Heavy footsteps. Running toward her. "No. No, no, no." Yana didn't want to look, but she had to. There were four guards sprinting across the parking lot toward her. Guards with guns. "I can't," she whispered. "I don't think I . . . I can't." She began to lower herself to the ground next to Sam. They'd have to get through her to get to him. She could do that much.

A car roared across the parking lot, squealing to a stop between Yana and the guards. The back door opened. Hands reached out. "Get in," someone cried. Yana couldn't. She couldn't.

But hands reached out and pulled her inside. Her and Sam. And the car drove away. Yana heard shots, but the car kept going. Out onto the street. Everything looked so strange. Like it was all part of a set for some play.

"Are you okay?" someone called.

"Rae. It's you," Yana said. "We're in Anthony's car."

"That's right. We're all here with you. Me and Anthony and Mandy," Rae answered, her voice slow and gentle. "We're going to take you to the hospital."

Hospital. Hospital. It took a moment for her to understand the word. "Not me. Sam! We've got to get Sam there."

"You and Sam," Rae promised.

Rae pounded into the emergency room, the two metal boxes slamming against her thighs. Yana wouldn't let her out of the car unless she brought them with her. "I've got a guy out in the car. Unconscious," she cried. "Breathed in a lot of smoke. A fire."

Before the last word was out of her mouth, a man and a woman in white were wheeling a stretcher out the glass door. Rae followed them to the car.

Anthony, Mandy, and Jesse were flanking the right passenger door. Through the window Rae could see Yana with the guy—Sam—cradled in her lap.

The woman in white opened the car door. "We need you to get out so we can help your friend," she told Yana.

Yana didn't seem to hear. Rae hurried over. She thrust the metal boxes at Anthony, then took Yana by the hand. It felt like a doll's hand, soft and pliant. "Come on, sweetie. They're going to take good care of Sam. But they can't reach him with you in the car." She gave Yana's hand a tug, and Yana obediently stepped out of the car. The ER team moved in fast. They had Sam strapped to the stretcher in moments. Yana ran after them as they wheeled the stretcher inside. Rae ran after her, not letting go of her hand.

"We need a crash cart," the man guiding the stretcher called as he wheeled Sam past the front desk. In a smooth motion he and the woman maneuvered the stretcher into a little cubicle. They drew the curtain behind them, blocking the stretcher from sight.

"Out of the way," a nurse called. She rushed by, pushing a metal cart in front of her. Rae caught a glimpse of dials and two plastic paddles. *Did his heart stop beating?* she wondered. *That's when you use the paddle things, isn't it?*

From behind the curtain Rae heard a voice yell, "Clear." Yana lunged forward and yanked open the curtain just in time to see Sam's body give a violent jerk. "You're hurting him!" Yana screeched.

"Please go to the waiting room," the nurse instructed. She pried Yana's fingers off the curtain and slid it shut again.

"Come on, Yana," Rae said. "We've got to let them help Sam."

"No." Yana shook her head. "No!"

"Clear!" a woman yelled from behind the curtain. Yana's body jerked. Just the way Rae imagined Sam's body was jerking on the stretcher. Several voices started talking at once behind the curtain. Then everyone went silent.

"Time of death. Ten-oh-seven," the man said.

"He's not dead!" Yana shouted. "Sam is not dead. He's not dying until Christmas." She ripped open the curtain, glaring at the medical team.

"Do you think . . . Could we have a minute. . . ." Rae gestured toward the body. God, the body.

"Just a minute," the nurse said. She squeezed Yana's arm as she led the other two medics out of the cubicle, then shut the curtain behind them.

"He's not dead," Yana repeated.

"Yan, I'm sorry, but he is," Rae answered, tears stinging her eyes. "Look at him."

Yana leaned over Sam's body and stared down at him. A tear splashed off her cheek and landed in one of his open, staring eyes. "No, he's alive."

She's lost it, Rae thought. *It's how I was with Aiden.* "Rae, touch his fingertips. You'll see. He's still in there."

"Good idea. Let me check. Let me make sure," Rae answered. If it would comfort Yana, she'd do it. She reached out her hand, turned Sam's hand palm up, and lightly rested her fingertips against his—

—and she found herself in a cage of wooden slats. Above her were clowns. Clowns dangling from strings. Tinkling music began to play, and the clowns began to spin in a circle above Rae, the polka dots and stripes of their costumes dizzying, their wide, smiling, red mouths almost menacing.

Remember why you're here. Remember why you're here, Rae ordered herself. "Sam!" she shouted. But the only sound was the tinkling music. The only motion was the circling clowns. Rae took a step forward. The floor was spongy under her feet. She knelt down and ran her fingers across the floor. *It's a mattress,* she thought. A second realization followed almost immediately—*I'm in a crib. A massive crib. And the clown, the clowns are a huge mobile.* Or else the crib and the mobile were regular size and Rae was tiny.

Doesn't matter which, Rae told herself. *You're in Sam's world. And if Sam's world still exists, then that means he's still alive. Right?* "Sam!" Rae yelled again. She ran across the mattress, sinking almost to her knees with each step. She reached the edge and—

—found herself at the top of a twisty metal slide. The ground looked a million miles away. And the metal looked slick, like it had been oiled. "Don't be afraid. You can do it," a voice that sounded like it belonged to a giant called.

Go! Rae urged herself. *Find Sam! Find Sam! Who knows how much time there is left!* She threw herself down on the side, stomach down, head rushing toward the earth, her body lurching left and right as she took the curves. She landed hard and felt—

—something cool and dry slither over her arm. A snake. She thought it was a boa constrictor. And it was a friend. Somehow she knew it was a friend. Natasha. That was its name. "Natasha, where's Sam?" she asked. The snake wriggled off her arm and slithered across the blacktop where Rae lay. She shoved herself to her feet and followed. Who knew a snake could move so fast? She pumped her legs harder. She had to keep up. Natasha would take her to Sam.

Yes! There he was. Leaping over the net of a tennis

court in the distance. "Sam! Sam, stop!" Rae yelled. Sam didn't hesitate. He kept running, running toward a blazing white sun. If he reached it, she'd die. No, he'd die. Would they both die?

No time to think, she ordered herself. *Just run.* Her lungs burned as she struggled to catch up to Sam. The blacktop under her feet turned slick and she went down—

—falling on top of a huge centerfold. The staples in the middle were as long as her arm. And the breasts on the model were like—who cared what they were like? Rae gained her feet again, searched frantically for Sam. He'd disappeared again.

No, he was still up ahead. A tiny dot against the blinding brightness of the sun. "Saaam!" Rae screeched. She plunged into a forest, a forest of syringes. Every few steps a bolt of electricity zigzagged through her body. But she couldn't stop running. The syringes grew closer together the farther she ran until they—

—formed a cage, blocking her in. *He's going to get away,* Rae thought. *Stop him!* She backed up as far as she could, then lowered her head. She pretended she was Anthony, Anthony on the football field. The syringes, they were the players on the other team. Her shoulders hit cold plastic. Rae didn't let herself hesitate. She plowed through. There was a cracking sound and rain, rain that burned like acid fell down on her, and she struggled—

—across the black and white squares of a chessboard, dodging the huge marble pieces that kept sliding in front of her, blocking her. But at least she could see Sam. He was almost to the edge of the other side of the board. So close. White, black, white, black.

Gray. Wait. The squares of the board were leaking together, becoming gray. The pieces were turning gray, too. The sky, gray. She glanced over her shoulder. All she saw was gray. In the distance Rae saw Sam's feet leave the ground. He was flying now, flying into the sun. If he got any closer . . .

"Nooo!" Rae shouted. "Turn around! Yana sent me to get you."

Sam fell from the sky, and Rae sprinted toward him, running faster than she'd run in any gym class ever. She dropped to her knees and skidded to a stop next to him. "Sam, we've got to get out of here. Yana's going to be so pissed if we don't get out of here."

Rae pulled Sam to his feet. Patches of his body had become the sun, shining so brightly, she could hardly look at him. She closed her eyes and jerked Sam back in the direction they'd come, then she plunged forward, dragging him behind her.

Cold. The air turned colder with every step. It was freezing her lungs. Freezing them flat. And her heart . . . It was slowing down. Cold. So cold. Too cold to beat any longer . . .

"When you touched the fingertips of a girl who was unconscious, you passed out," a familiar voice said. "What in the hell did you think would happen if you touched the fingertips of a dead guy?"

Rae opened her eyes. Anthony's face filled her vision, big as the sun. Warming her. "I'm alive?"

He leaned down and kissed her, hard, his lips urgent against hers. "Yes, you're alive," he answered when he lifted his mouth from hers. "But you might not have been."

Rae struggled to sit up and found that she was on a gurney. Anthony put his hands on her shoulders and tried to guide her back down. "The doctor said for you to rest."

"I'm fine." Rae gripped the rails of the gurney with both hands, resisting him. "What happened to Sam?"

"His heart started beating again. Totally freaked the doctors out," Anthony answered. He pushed Rae's sweaty hair off her face. "It's thanks to you. You know that."

Rae shook her head. "We made it out because we

knew how pissed Yana would be if we didn't." She ran her fingers down Anthony's cheek. "And because I could never leave you. You know that, right? You're stuck with me."

"I guess I can deal with that," Anthony muttered. "Since I love you and all that."

"That's right." Rae looped her arms around his neck. "You love me, and that means you're mine. So help me down."

"The doctor said—" Anthony began.

"Since when do you listen to anybody?" Rae asked. "I'm fine."

Anthony caught her under her knees, lifted her over the railing of the gurney, and gently set her on her feet. He didn't let go of her waist. She kept her arms tight around his shoulders. They were RaeAnthony, AnthonyRae, and she wanted to keep it that way. "Take me to Sam," she said.

And he walked her down the hall, his steps and her steps perfectly in sync because they really only had one body, one mind, one heart.

"She's supposed to be resting," Yana said as they entered Sam's room.

"Yeah," Mandy said. Rae noticed her fingers were tightly twined with Jesse's. They weren't MandyJesse. Not yet. But maybe someday, if they were lucky, as lucky as she and Anthony . . .

"You know Rae. She doesn't listen to anybody but Rae," Anthony answered.

"Hey, I . . ." Sam frowned at Rae. "I had a dream, and you were in it."

"It wasn't exactly a dream," Rae answered.

"Sam, this is Rae. She's one of us," Yana said. "So's Mandy." She nodded in Mandy's direction.

"More guinea pigs," Sam muttered.

"No," Yana said firmly. "No. We're nobody's guinea pigs. And we're not gonna be. I burned down the center, the whole thing."

"Pretty good for a guinea pig," Sam answered.

What's with this guinea pig stuff? Rae wondered. But she didn't interrupt to ask. Things between Yana and Sam were so intense, Rae could practically feel heat waves coming off them.

"But it's not over. You know that," Sam added.

Yana let out a sigh that sounded like it came from the soles of her feet. "Yeah, I know that. When these guys rescued me"—she made a sweeping gesture that took in Rae, Anthony, Mandy, and Jesse—"there were already new agency goons coming for me." She scrubbed her face with her fingers. "Maybe I didn't do anything. Maybe I—"

God, she suddenly sounded so deflated. Like all the energy and all the life had been sucked out of her.

"Your mom would be proud of you," Rae interrupted.

"She wanted to close down the agency—that's why they killed her. And now you're fighting them, too. Just like her."

"And we're going to keep on fighting," Anthony told her.

"All of us," Mandy added.

"All of us," Jesse echoed.

Yana's face softened, and Rae got a glimpse of what Yana must have looked like as a little girl, that little girl who wanted to be a ballerina. "Thanks, you guys," she said softly. "After what I did to you, I—"

"We've all done stupid things," Anthony cut Yana off. Rae pulled him more tightly against her.

"What about you, Sam?" Yana asked. "You showed up at the center tonight, even though you told me there was no way you'd help. Are you in?"

"Yeah. I'm in. I'm in until I'm out, whenever that will be. I can't promise you anything but that," Sam answered.

Yana nodded, and Rae saw that her blue eyes were bright with unshed tears. "That's good enough for me. More than good enough." A grin slowly spread across her face. "And I did manage to snag something that will slow the agency down."

"What?" Rae asked.

"Samples of a new drug called N-Tetran. It'll boost all of our powers," Yana answered.

"It'll take the agency months, at the least months, to re-create the formula," Sam said. "We'll definitely have an advantage for a while."

"So the agency better start watching its butt," Yana said. She met Rae's gaze. "Because together, even without the drug, we've kicked some butt."

"And we're going to keep on kicking it," Rae agreed. She reached out and took Yana's hand. "Together."

Turn the page for a sneak peek at another great series from HarperCollins:

THE WESSEX PAPERS

Volume 1

TRUST FALLS

available June 2002

1

I should be wearing a dominatrix outfit. With stiletto heels. And a clown nose.

These were Sunday Winthrop's first thoughts as Mom and Dad hustled her out of the afternoon sunshine and into the dark foyer of Headmaster Olsen's mansion.

Well actually that wasn't quite true. These were her *second* thoughts. Her first thought was that somebody should finally suggest to Headmaster Olsen that he give up on the comb-over. Gently, of course. The poor guy. She tried to smile as she shook his hand. Oh, the humanity. She'd watched him fight a desperate battle with male pattern baldness for—what, now? Fifteen years?

"How are you, Sunday?"

"Fine, thanks, Mr. Olsen. And you?"

"Oh, same as always. Heh, heh, heh."

He wasn't lying. Sunday had been barely two years old when Dad brought her here for the first time—for his fifteenth reunion. (Yikes. That meant Dad's *thirtieth* reunion was this fall. Which meant another alumni bash from hell. Was it too late to apply for an exchange program in Siberia?) In the intervening years, Dad had matured into a happy-go-lucky, graying, Richard Gere-type. Mom had discovered hobbies, like watercolor painting. Sunday herself had become a young woman, complete with cleavage. But Olsen hadn't changed a bit, except for the loss of a few more hairs. He still had that ruddy face. That bow tie. Those beige slacks. Not pants. *Slacks.* That wide-wale corduroy jacket . . .

But back to the stilettos and clown nose.

The problem was this: The moment Sunday walked in the door, she saw that Allison was wearing the exact same Lily Pulitzer dress as she was. Now normally Sunday would laugh at this kind of snafu. ("Oh, look," somebody was sure to say. "How cute. Sunday and Allison are wearing the same outfit. Just like when they were kids!") But Allison had called Sunday the night before, for the express purpose of avoiding such a coincidence:

Allison: "So what are you going to wear at Olsen's tomorrow?"

Sunday: "Not sure yet. I was thinking about that Lily Pulitzer dress."

Allison: "The one I have?"

Sunday: "Yeah? Why? Are you going to wear it?"

Allison: "Oh, no. Too conservative."

Sunday: "You think so?"

Allison: "Definitely. I want to make a splash. It *is* the first day of senior year."

Yet there Allison was, in Olsen's living room—standing solo among the plates of hors d'oeuvres and the shelves full of leather-bound books . . . in the Lily Pulitzer. Right by the rolltop desk. On the first day of senior year. Classic. Sunday shook her head. *Splash, my ass.* She knew exactly what Allison had been thinking. Oh, yes. She knew the Allison strategy from a lifetime of experience. Allison had been planning on wearing the Lily Pulitzer from the get-go. So she'd made a preemptive strike. She wanted Sunday to *doubt* the Lily Pulitzer. To make Sunday think that it *was* a little too conservative. To play on Sunday's fashion insecurities. And when Sunday went with the splash herself, Allison would counterstrike with the Lily. . . .

Whatever. It was funny. It was ridiculous, actually. Sunday knew she shouldn't get angry, because getting angry was something Allison would do. She should appreciate the silliness of it all. Hey, at least she didn't look like Nicole Kidman. At least she had her own thing going: skinny frame, long dark hair, no immediate celebrity resemblances. Allison's resemblance to Nicole Kidman was terrifying, right down to that little button nose. She was a full-fledged clone. (Oddly enough, though, Allison spoke like Madonna, post-elocution lessons—thanks to years of etiquette camp. Her accent fell somewhere between JFK and the Queen of England.)

"Aren't you going to go say hi to Allison, honey?" Dad asked.

No, thanks.

"She's standing all by herself," Mom said.

Maybe she forgot to wear deodorant.

"Oh, look!" Headmaster Olsen exclaimed. "You two have the same dress. How cute!"

Sunday smiled. "It is cute, isn't it?" she said.

Allison pretended not to notice them. This was a fairly difficult feat, considering that she was less than fifteen feet away—and alone. But she doggedly chewed on a stuffed mushroom and stared at a spot on the wall just above Olsen's antique globe. The "lost-in-thought" look, Sunday supposed. God help them all. Where was Mackenzie, anyway?

"The party's out back," Olsen said. "Come, come. Let's have a drink, shall we?"

"Is Mackenzie out there?" Sunday asked.

"No, I'm afraid the Wildes aren't here yet," Olsen said. He whisked Mom and Dad into the living room, heading for the back door. "Oh, that reminds me. Thanks for your timely submission for the time capsule! Mackenzie hasn't sent hers in yet. . . ."

"Hi, Allison!" Mom called.

Sunday's smile became strained.

"Oh, hi, Mr. and Mrs. Winthrop!" Allison shook her head and smiled as they hurried past her. "I didn't see you."

Dad jerked his head toward Sunday before disappearing around the corner. "Look who's here," he cried jovially. "Roomie number two!"

Thanks, Dad. Thanks for reminding me.

Allison turned to her. Her own fake smile faltered—just for an instant. Then she started grinding her teeth.

"Hey, what do you know?" Sunday said. "We wore the same dress. Maybe Mackenzie will, too. Then we'll be like sisters. Triplets."

"Right," Allison said. She seemed confused.

Sunday swallowed. Now came the hard part.

Did they do the "hello hug," or didn't they?

There was really no reason to do the hello hug. Sunday had seen Allison only a week ago, out in East Hampton. The hello hug was usually reserved for seeing a dear friend after a long time. A month or more. On the other hand, they *had* done the hello hug every year so far at Olsen's annual AB Welcome Party. It was a ritual. It was *formal.* And that was the kicker: Allison was big on formalities. So she'd probably go for it.

Then again . . . maybe she wouldn't. Maybe she could sense Sunday's hesitation. Or maybe the embarrassment over the dress would preempt the hello hug.

All right, worst case scenario: Sunday would go for the hello hug, and Allison would hesitate, and then Sunday would hesitate, too—and they'd end up in some kind of awkward little *non-hug* which they would both try to laugh off, making the whole thing that much more excruciating. . . .

Why is my life so very, very lame?

Sunday smiled at Allison. Allison smiled back. The seconds ticked by.

"You look pretty, Sun," Allison said.

"You too, Al," Sunday replied.

"Thanks." Allison nodded toward the tray table of stuffed mushrooms. "You should try those. They're really good."

And that settled it. Sigh of relief. Allison had deftly guided them into the midst of a conversation, bypassing opening pleasantries, so there was no longer any need for the hello hug. Nor, apparently, was there any need to talk further about the dress. *Well done, Al,* Sunday silently congratulated her. *Well done.*

"So how come you're not outside with everyone else?" she asked, heading straight for the mushrooms.

"I'm waiting for Hobson," Allison said. "We're supposed to discuss something."

Sunday suppressed a grin. Hobson was Allison's boyfriend. His full name was Mortimer Hobson Crowe III. Allison had been going out with him since sophomore year. He was tall, blond, and blue-eyed. He sort of looked like a cross between the *Dawson's Creek* guy and a young Robert Redford. He had what people used to call "moneyed good looks." Members of his family had been at Wessex for five generations, earning him the longest lineage of any AB.

Ergo: He was Allison's ideal mate. *Was* being the key word.

Last year, however, he came down with a severe case of IFTHS (I'm-From-The-Hood Syndrome). The symptoms were sudden and baffling, as they often are. He'd started wearing a black wool hat. His baggy pants hung low. He flashed signs for nonexistent gangs. His friends became his "dawgs." Everything he said came in a "yo" sandwich; all utterances began and ended with "yo." (Example: "Yo, where my dawgs at, yo?") He even took to writing his own raps, referring to himself as "Sir Mack-A-Lot."

"*Yo, you know I rock a party in style.*

Sir Mack-A-Lot's here to get buck wild. . . ."

IFTHS was fairly common, of course. Sunday figured it struck about one out of every five white males at some point or another, to some degree. Even at Wessex it had reached the proportions of a minor epidemic. Still, this was the first time it had ever happened to a good friend, an AB—one of their own. And Hobson seemed like the unlikeliest candidate of all. He was from New Canaan, for God's sake. His mother used to dress him in a little sailor's uniform.

Still, the condition did have its upsides. The most beautiful and demented of these was that Allison refused to acknowledge that any change had taken place. Almost overnight, Mortimer Hobson Crowe III had become the latest hip-hop sensation (in his own mind), but Allison pretended not to notice. Having a "homey" for a boyfriend simply wasn't part of her Seven-Part Life Plan. People would rag on him; she would brush them off. As far as Allison was concerned, Hobson had to be perfect, so he *was* perfect. Case closed.

Hobson, to his credit, always took the heat with the same good-natured reply: "Yo, whatever, I'm keepin' it real, yo." *Keepin' it real*. How? By not tucking his shirt in? Everyone laughed behind his back—or to his face—but he didn't seem to care. He actually seemed to have fun with it. He would make Allison mix tapes. She would go out of her way to tell Sunday and Mackenzie how sweet he was. The tapes were filled with songs like "Big Pimpin'" and "I Want a Gangsta Bitch." Sunday wished more than anything that she could videotape their conversations when they were alone. Maybe Hobson called Allison his "Gangsta Bitch." For all Sunday knew, it went both ways. Maybe Allison called him her "Big Pimp."

"This is so typical," Allison muttered under her breath.

"What is?" Sunday asked, reaching for a mushroom.

"He refuses to discuss what we're going to wear to the Harvest Ball."

"But that isn't until October," Sunday said.

Allison frowned at her. "That's exactly what *he* said. The point is, I wanted to discuss it with him *now*—with his parents present—so Mrs. Crowe will know the specific brand of cummerbund I want him to wear with his tuxedo. I was planning for it to match my dress—"

Hobson suddenly burst through the kitchen door, nearly tripping on the tattered hem of his pants. All his clothes were at least two sizes too big.

He froze when he saw them. His eyes bulged. He gave them both a once-over.

"Damn, yo!" he cried gleefully. "Wassup, dawgs? Those dresses are *ill*." He shook his head and grabbed a handful of mushrooms, stuffing them into his mouth at once. "Y'all look like a Doublemint commercial."

Sunday grinned. Sweet, sweet Hobson. "You hear that, Al?" she asked. "We look like a Doublemint commercial."

Allison didn't answer. She was busy grinding her teeth again.

An hour later, when Mackenzie finally showed up, Sunday had somehow managed to get herself cornered by Headmaster Olsen and Winslow Ellis—"Winnie"—in the backyard.

Being stuck with Olsen wouldn't have been *so* bad. True, he was going on and on about the varsity basketball team, a subject in which Sunday had about as much interest as, say, any other sport—but there was something cute about his excitement. It was so *genuine.* Sunday's father had played basketball for Wessex, so Olsen naturally assumed that Sunday would be thrilled about the new talent coming in this year, some whiz from Washington, D.C. . . .That was the defining feature of Olsen's personality: He honestly believed that ABs were younger versions of their parents. Chips off the old block, as it were.

Winnie, on the other hand . . . *Blecch.* Talk about the antithesis of genuine. Everything about him was fake. Well, except for his suit: It was made of summer wool. But that was it. Even his *body* was fake. The guy had clearly undergone some major reconstructive surgery over the summer. The dark caterpillar on his forehead had been severed and trimmed, leaving him two perfect eyebrows. His nose was smaller, too. And his chin looked more pointy. Sadly, though, the surgeons couldn't do anything about his blubbery hips. Or the rest of his body hair. (Actually, it was closer to fur.) Maybe

Winnie would have to wait until he was older for the electrolysis and liposuction. Or maybe Olsen wanted him to stay fat; Winnie was the basketball team's center, and Olsen was saying something about a big presence in the middle. . . .

"That's what it's going to take to beat Carnegie Mansion in the exhibition game," Winnie confirmed. "Defense. Strong defense."

Olsen nodded. "That's true. But the best defense, as we well know, is a good *offense.*"

The two of them chuckled.

"So is this new kid . . ." Winnie snapped his fingers.

"Fred Wright."

"Yes. Is this Fred Wright *really* that good?"

Olsen nodded. "He can carry an entire game if called upon."

Who on earth cares? Sunday's smile grew pained. Olsen's cuteness was rapidly wearing thin. She could feel herself starting to get panicky. *This is my future,* she realized. Yes, this was as good as it was going to get, as far as senior year went: getting stuck with Olsen and Winnie at lame AB functions and being forced to pretend to listen to them. *My God.* The boredom was lethal. Wasn't there was a Greek myth about that? Yeah, there was . . . it was about a king who was bored to death by a dull story. What was his name? Her retention was so lousy when it came to history. . . .

Thankfully, at that moment Mackenzie swooped in and yanked Sunday out of the conversation.

"Something's going on between Al and Hobson," Mackenzie whispered urgently, dragging Sunday across the manicured lawn toward the back door of the mansion. "Something big. I heard them fighting. I *knew* it. I checked all of our star charts this morning—you know, first day of senior year and all—and guess what the horoscope said? Leos are supposed to watch out for 'confrontation in their love lives.'" She made little quotation marks in the air with her fingers.

Sunday smiled. Ah, Mackenzie. Sunday never had to worry about a worst case hello-hug scenario with Mackenzie. The girl's social skills were nonexistent. It was one of the greatest things about her: She was too wrapped up in the world of star charts and horoscopes and her friends' futures to be awkward or even polite. Especially when it came to good gossip. Anything going on between Hobson and Allison was bound to be entertaining. As long as Mom and Dad didn't see them making an escape . . .

"Where are you going, honey?" Dad called.

But of course, they would.

Sunday glanced over her shoulder. "To get some more stuffed mushrooms," she answered.

Dad grinned crookedly. He seemed to be swaying a bit. He was clutching an empty plastic cup in one hand. "Did you hear the news?"

"About the basketball team?" Sunday asked.

He laughed. "No, no—about your chair. They found the chair that I had when I was a student here!"

Sunday hesitated, still smiling. She had no idea how she was supposed to respond to that statement. *The chair?*

"Get this," he added. "You know how they knew it was mine? I'd carved my initials in the seat. Back then, that would have gotten me expelled. But now it's a piece of nostalgia. Like the time capsule! Ha! Anyway, it was in room two-oh-three in Ellis Hall, and they took it out and gave it to you. . . ."

Best just to leave. Dad was clearly floundering in the sea of Olsen's cocktails. He was still talking, in fact, as Sunday pushed Mackenzie through the door into the kitchen.

" . . . real piece of history . . ."

"How many V&Ts has he had?" Mackenzie asked, giggling.

"I'd say three," Sunday muttered. "So where are they?"

"Upstairs."

Sunday followed her, snaking her way through Olsen's first floor—through all the little corridors, past all the Colonial knickknacks and paintings of various Wessex buildings. They were all done by artists who had attended the school, no doubt. The wooden floorboards creaked under their feet. For about the hundredth time, Sunday realized how absolutely perfect this house was for Olsen. It was a portrait of him. It was stodgy, cute, and it never changed.

"Hey, speaking of Ellis Hall, where's Noah?" Mackenzie whispered. "He always makes me laugh at these parties."

Sunday grinned. "Noah Percy makes you laugh because he's a total freak."

"Oh, come on," Mackenzie said. "You *love* Noah."

That was true, actually. Sunday did love Noah—precisely because he *was* a total freak. Also, he had a major crush on her. Being around him was always good for a boost in the old self-esteem department.

"But can you believe that Noah *chose* to live in Ellis?" Mackenzie whispered. "I mean, Mr. Burwell lives there. That guy was *definitely* a serial killer in his past life."

Sunday shrugged. "Noah's always been a glutton for punishment."

Mackenzie paused at the bottom of the stairwell. She glanced over her shoulder, a serious expression on her face. "Shh," she whispered.

"Gotcha." Sunday bit her lip to keep from laughing.

Mackenzie started tiptoeing up the stairs.

Sunday followed as quietly as possible. The floorboards were creaking again. Mackenzie paused at the top of the landing and pointed to a door at the end of the hall: Olsen's bedroom. It was open—just a crack. Two muffled voices drifted out into the hall. Sunday strained her ears.

" . . . don't understand it," Allison said with a sniffle.

Sunday's smile vanished. Wow. Allison actually sounded *sad.* This *was* a big deal.

"Yo, Al—why you buggin'?" Hobson asked. "You know we got to end this. A playa's got to be free."

Wait a second, Sunday thought. She stared at Mackenzie. *Is Hobson—*

"But what about the Harvest Ball?" Allison shrieked. "Or forget about the Harvest Ball, what about the Gold and Silver? We already have tickets! And reservations at the Plaza! You can't do this to me—"

"Come on, Al. We can't stay together just to go to some party. That's like . . . like Eric B. & Rakim getting back together just to do a reunion concert. It's kinda wack, yo. You gotta do it for the *looove.* For real. Know what I'm sayin'?"

Sunday's eyes widened.

Mackenzie cupped her hands over her mouth.

Oh my God. Hobson was dumping Allison. This was big. This was *huge.* The poor girl! Talk about a major, major crimp in the Seven-Part Life Plan . . .

Mackenzie tugged on Sunday's sleeve, then hurried back downstairs.

Sunday frowned. Where was she going? This was just getting good.

"Come on," Mackenzie mouthed. "We shouldn't be listening to this."

For a moment, Sunday stood there. Why shouldn't they be listening? This was the kind of once-in-a-lifetime gossip that would keep the Wessex rumor mill churning for years. And they were the first ones on the scene. . . .

Then she sighed.

Okay. Mackenzie felt sorry for Allison. Of course she did. Mackenzie was *nice.* And Sunday supposed that she felt sorry for Allison, too. After all, the girl had put all her eggs in the Sir Mack-A-Lot basket, and now that basket had been tossed into the proverbial recycling bin.

Deep down, though, Sunday had to admit to something: Witnessing this breakup mostly made her feel sorry for herself. Yes—it was pitiful but true. Because Allison was having one of those defining, life-changing, senior-quote moments. A time-capsule moment. And that meant a lot. At the very least, Allison had known *some* romance in the recent past. She'd known *some* drama. *Some* love.

Sunday, on the other hand, hadn't had a boyfriend since the tenth grade. She hadn't even kissed anyone . . . not since Boyce Sutton had tried to unbutton her shirt and she'd slapped him in the face—simultaneously ending their relationship and earning herself a reputation as a huge prude among Boyce's friends. That was *her* last bit of drama: She'd been labeled a nun.

Of course, she couldn't care less about what Boyce's friends thought about her. Well, except maybe for Carter Boyce. He was kind of cute. But his last name was the same as Boyce's first name, and that could get a little weird; if they ever got together, it might be like fooling around with Boyce's brother or something.

Actually, that wasn't weird. No. What was weird was that there were only about five guys at Wessex whom she could possibly date without majorly freaking out her friends and family, and two of them—nearly half—were named "Boyce" in one way or another.

But it was best not to think about that. It was too depressing.